Five Pieces of Jade

JOHN BALL

"Recall *In the Heat of the Night?* Mr. Ball is as good, if not better, in the cool of the day."
—*Boston Herald Traveler*

"A first-rate writer who lends authenticity to his work by incorporating an unusual understanding of police investigative techniques . . . don't miss *Five Pieces of Jade.*"
—*Richmond News Leader*

"Well written and fast-paced . . . a delight to read."
—*Jackson Sun*

Five Pieces of Jade

JOHN BALL

PERENNIAL LIBRARY
Harper & Row, Publishers
New York, Cambridge, Philadelphia, San Francisco
London, Mexico City, São Paulo, Singapore, Sydney

A hardcover edition of this book was published by Little, Brown & Company. It is here reprinted by arrangement with the author.

FIVE PIECES OF JADE. Copyright © 1972 by John Ball. All rights reserved. Printed in the United States of America. No part of this book may be used or reproduced in any manner whatsoever without written permission except in the case of brief quotations embodied in critical articles and reviews. For information address Dominick Abel Literary Agency, Inc., 498 West End Avenue, New York, N.Y. 10024. Published simultaneously in Canada by Fitzhenry & Whiteside Limited, Toronto.

First PERENNIAL LIBRARY edition published 1985.

Library of Congress Cataloging in Publication Data

Ball, John Dudley, 1911–
    Five pieces of jade.

    I. Title. II. Title: 5 pieces of jade.
PS3552.A455F5   1985   813'.54   84-48578
ISBN 0-06-080752-0 (pbk.)

85   86   87   88   89   10   9   8   7   6   5   4   3   2   1

For Gwyneth and Peter Bealer

Author's Note

Great assistance in the preparation of this book was rendered by the Pasadena, California, Police Department, particularly by Chief Robert McGowan, Agents Floyd Sanderson and James Garner, and a number of Virgil Tibbs' fellow investigators.

Mr. Frank Larkworthy of the Federal Bureau of Narcotics and Dangerous Drugs was an invaluable source of information over an extended period. Major help was also given by the Los Angeles Police Department, particularly by Commander Charles Reese; Captain Jack Wilson; Captain Donald Wesley, the commander of the Narcotics Investigation Division; and by Sergeant John Odom, whose vast experience in the field was of great value.

In the area of illicit drug merchandising and addiction, expert assistance was given by Messrs. Phinis S. Willis, Arthur Walker, Jr., and Hugh Stack, all of whom are highly knowledgeable in this field.

A number of jade authorities were most generous with their time and knowledge. Among them, and deserving of special mention, are Mr. Norman Lee of the Jin Hing Company, Los Angeles; Mr. James Wei, Director of Information for the Republic of China; Mr. Goh Keng Tong of the Moongate, Singapore; and Mr. Robert Loh of the same establishment.

Lastly, Mr. Tibbs has asked me to express his gratitude to all those who have taken an interest in his work. He has suggested that his reported cases should be considered not as personal achievements, but rather as representative of what is continuously being done by police officers everywhere.

JOHN BALL

Five Pieces of Jade

CHAPTER *1*

Yumeko did not need to open the draperies that covered the large front window to look down the street; she simply drew back one corner and put her head close to the glass. In fact the draperies were seldom opened because Mr. Wang preferred to have them closed. And since it was Mr. Wang's house, and he was the master of it in the fullest sense of the word, they continued to shut out both the bright light of day and the view of neighbors who might display undue curiosity concerning what was going on inside.

Far down the street, making his slow way closer, she saw the mailman. His stubby little vehicle, she knew, would be filled with information, news, and some goods which he would mete out in small portions along the length of his route. Much of what he had would be either routine or unwanted; the remainder would be the vital part, good news and bad already at least a day or two old, but which would not become known until the delivery had been completed. Yumeko had little anticipation of her own. It was because of Mr. Wang that she was anxious for the man in the red, white, and blue vehicle to reach their driveway and give them what was theirs. What he did after that was no concern of hers, at least not for another twenty-four hours.

What she did not like was having to go outside to collect the mail. She did not care to appear in public, even on the streets of this quiet West Coast American city. She was twenty-six years old and in some respects quite beautiful; her face was well formed and her dark Asiatic eyes needed no makeup to exert an exotic fascination. Her body, in most respects, was all that she could reasonably hope for. She had a natural liquid grace which set off well the contours of her figure and, unlike many girls born in the Far East, she had both well-proportioned legs and a very satisfactory bosom according to American standards. But she still kept out of sight as much as she was able — people asked too many questions.

She waited until the postman was slowing up in front of the house. Then she went out, her eyes protesting the sudden brilliance of the sunlight. The mailman knew her, which in a way was a small help. She accepted from him a small handful of envelopes, none of which appeared too important, and then waited. When he turned to look behind him she was suddenly hopeful. Then he got out, opened the rear door, and extracted a box.

Yumeko signed for it on behalf of Mr. Wang and took it carefully into her arms. It was moderately heavy, as she had hoped it would be. Attached to it was a brown envelope which contained the necessary documents; it had been opened and resealed with Scotch tape. Walking carefully to guard against a last-minute disaster, she reentered the house, put the package down in the center of the marble-topped table in the foyer, and then went to inform Mr. Wang that at long last the shipment he had waited for so patiently had arrived.

Wang Fu-sen looked up pleasantly when she came into his study; he almost always did that no matter what the hour or whatever state of mind he might be in. It was as though he were trying to erase all of the unhappy moments in her past life, despite the fact that he had already given her far more than anyone could possibly be expected to do. "The mail just came," she said. "There is a package from Singapore."

Mr. Wang blinked once or twice behind his rimless glasses. "How does it appear?" he asked.

"I saw no signs of damage."

"Excellent." He rose from his desk and came forward. Because he had no intention of going out that day, and was expecting no visitors, he was wearing the long dark purple Chinese gown that he favored for his days at home. "Please bring the box into the kitchen."

Dutifully she went and collected it, carrying it for the last few feet of its long journey with a full sense of its importance. Her slender knowledge could never match the vast learning of Mr. Wang concerning the stone of heaven, but since she had been living in his house her interest had been awakened and he had helped her with his instruction.

Although he was over seventy years of age, Mr. Wang's hands were still smooth and capable. With them he cut the cord which surrounded the wrapping paper, then removed the paper itself with the neat skill of the careful craftsman. When he had finished, a plain wooden box was revealed, addressed on the outside so that if the paper had been torn away, it could still have found its destination. For just a few moments Mr. Wang examined the documents which had been in the brown envelope and found them all in order. The Certificate of Antiquity was the most important; it verified the contents and in so doing made them admissible into the United States, duty free. It was not the duty which concerned Mr. Wang, but for a long time there had been a ban; during that period the certificates had been absolutely essential.

With a light hammer and a screwdriver he carefully removed the twenty-two small nails which held the lid in place. When he had done so, he lifted it away and saw a carefully compressed mass of excelsior. Buried within it there was another box, this one also wrapped in brown paper. As soon as Mr. Wang had lifted it out, Yumeko removed the outer box and the wrappings, putting them neatly to one side. Her anticipation almost matched Mr. Wang's as he unwrapped the paper and at last revealed a cloth-covered blue box that was held shut by two ivory pins that fitted into sleeves.

Before he opened the box Mr. Wang deliberately waited while Yumeko swept the tabletop clear with her hands and dropped the stray pieces of excelsior into the wastebasket. Then he slipped out the ivory pins and lifted the lid.

The entire inside was lined with white satin. On the lid it had been formed into a cushion; in the bottom it carefully nestled a crudely shaped implement of stone. The object was no more than an inch wide and very slightly tapered, in length something between nine and ten inches. As Yumeko looked at it she was disappointed in its color; it was a dirty light gray and in a few places the edges had been crystalized so that they appeared ready to crumble. When she looked into the face of Mr. Wang as he contemplated it, she knew that once more her superficial feminine judgment had been wrong.

"I am very grateful that it has arrived safely," she said.

Mr. Wang wiped his glasses. "You are wise, for if anything had happened to it, no replacement would have been possible. You understand what it is?"

"It is jade."

"Indeed yes, but that is like saying that Lao-tzu was a man. It is a true *Ya-Chang*, which in ancient China authorized the bearer to mobilize troops or to take command of important military installations. There are many fakes, but this one is genuine. Can you estimate its age?"

Yumeko looked at it again and knew that it was very old indeed; it had probably been made before Christ was born. "Han Dynasty?" she ventured.

Mr. Wang smiled at her with gentle regard. "That is most intelligent; it could very well be Western Han, and it shows indications of that period. However, there are certain small details which, when it was examined by experts, established that it is earlier still. It is accepted to be of the Chou Dynasty, most likely the Period of the Spring and Summer Annuals."

She studied it for a moment before she spoke again. "It is most fortunate that it is now in your hands."

Graciously Mr. Wang bowed to her. "Your speech is as well made as the beauty that surrounds you."

"I am not beautiful." She said it tersely, unwilling even for a moment to forget the thing she could never leave behind her.

The one man who had been truly kind to her in her life lifted his hand. "Let us install the precious *Ya-Chang*."

As he picked up the box she ran ahead to turn on the lights. Despite the harsh sunlight outside, the well-protected large room at the rear of the house would be in darkness. It was a tribute to the trust that Mr. Wang reposed in her that she was allowed to visit it at any time and to remain as long as she liked. With proper feminine instinct, which did not betray her this time, she left the main lights off and pressed the switch for the cabinet lights instead.

The room came to life, revealing a spectacle difficult to match in the Western world. Against all four walls glass-fronted cabinets displayed a spectacular array of exquisite carvings; there were standing beauties in graceful postures holding flowers, trays, and ritual objects. There were vases, incense burners, jars intertwined by leaves and flowers frozen in perpetual beauty, several *Pi* discs mounted vertically in intricately carved wooden stands. There were recognizable animals and fabulous creatures that had lived only in legend and mythology. A unicorn raised his head in defiant urgency; next to him a catlike creature crouched ready to spring. Delicate bowls stood in serene beauty, so thin that the concealed lighting was visible through their sides. Almost every color known to nature created a phantasmagoric world; the whole effect was breathtaking, even to those who had seen it without any knowledge of the wealth of tradition and culture that it represented.

From beneath his gown Mr. Wang produced a ring of keys, and unlocked the cabinet which contained the earliest antiques. A place had already been prepared for the ancient badge of office. Lifting it for the first time from its cushioned box, he placed it carefully into position and stepped back to inspect the results. Satisfied, he relocked the case and then led the way into the living room. Yumeko followed after she had turned off the lights and secured the door, aware that her benefactor wished to speak further with her.

In a manner that was a fortunate compromise between East and West Mr. Wang seated himself in an upholstered chair and motioned to Yumeko to make herself comfortable. When she had done so, he placed his arms formally on the sides of his chair and addressed her. "It is many months now since you first came here. I wish to say that each day you have been in my home, you have filled it with an empathy which has brought me much happiness."

Yumeko lowered her head, but understood she was not to interrupt his discourse.

"It is my acute misfortune to have reached an age where I can regard you only as something precious to behold."

"But still, people talk." She thought she saw what was coming and she wanted desperately to forestall it.

"My dear, there is nothing more futile in life than concerning oneself about what people think. It is more to the point to let them worry about how you regard them. Persons who observe others' affairs condemn themselves. Ignore them; it is what they most deserve and at the same time the punishment they are least prepared to endure."

"I will remember your wisdom."

Mr. Wang continued. "Despite the fact that you have been out of this house very little, you have greatly improved your knowledge of the language and of the nature of this country. It is now my wish that you abandon your seclusion and begin to build a social life for yourself."

Yumeko bowed her head. "I can deny you nothing," she said. "But what you are asking of me is beyond what I can endure. It is best that I go back where I came from."

Slowly Mr. Wang shook his head. "You have one life to live here on this earth, the rest is uncertain. You cannot throw it away. Some things are beyond our powers to change, in that case they must be endured. I am of the opinion that you will find your burdens to be much less than you envision them."

She knew he was not withdrawing his support from her; rather he was doing something which he conceived of as being for her own good. And in that respect he had never been wrong. The more graciously she accepted his decision, the more respect she could show him and all that he had done for her in the past.

"Shall I seek employment?" she asked.

"It has already been arranged for you. I am fortunate in having a valued friend who operates a wholesale travel business. He is in need of someone who is fluent in Japanese and English and who can write both languages. You possess those qualifications. An interview will be unnecessary; he was kind enough to accept the judgment of someone as ill-qualified as myself."

Yumeko lowered her head; she did not ask the question that was in the forefront of her mind because it could have only one answer — her prospective employer knew who and what she was. "I am pleased to do as you wish. I hope I may do you honor."

Mr. Wang smiled at her. "You have always done that. I trust that you will return as often as you find it convenient to my poor house and brighten it with your presence."

She looked at him quickly and tightened her small hands into fists. "I do not wish to leave you, sir. Please allow me to continue to live here."

Again he raised his hand, a gesture which commanded her to silence. When he spoke, the tones of his voice took on a new gentleness and understanding of her position. "To have you remain here would grant my dearest wish, but I cannot permit it. There are several reasons, but one overshadows the rest."

"Please do not tell me that it is for my own good," Yumeko pleaded.

Mr. Wang smiled at her. "I shall not do that. It is another matter entirely. There are forces of which you have no understanding which presently surround me. When our forebears, yours and mine, spoke of evil spirits, it was of such as are pressing me now."

She tightened her hands until the knuckles went white. "Are you in any danger?"

"Danger is not easily defined. I have taken certain precautions, but it will come anyway. When it does, it may be a very little thing. Even if it is no more than that, I do not want you to be involved."

"But you could be in actual danger," she persisted.

Once more he lifted an eloquent hand. "I beg of you, dismiss it from your mind. A very small wind seldom blows out the candle, even if the flame is already faltering."

CHAPTER 2

Although his office was comfortably air-conditioned, Chief Robert McGowan of the Pasadena Police Department could almost feel the midsummer heat outside. The brilliant California sun baked the window glass and burned hard patterns onto the carpeting. It was proving to be a hot summer indeed, and there were many who, in their way, were trying to make it hotter still.

Bob McGowan sat with his long frame twisted sideways in his chair and his feet stretched across an open lower drawer of his desk. While he clarified his thoughts he studied an attractive bamboolike plant that was growing with airy grace in a pot on his windowsill. Few of the visitors to his office who admired it knew that it was marijuana. Downstairs in the narcotics division there was a considerable collection of other exhibits, some of them less than pleasant, that were kept on hand for educational and training purposes.

McGowan had been selected for his job because, among other things, he had a decided gift for communicating with people: those who worked for him and those in the community whom he served. When the retirement of Chief Addis had opened up the top spot a few months previously, there had been several outstanding candidates from within the Pasadena Police Department. He had been picked because at that time there had been a slowly growing anatagonism between the police authorities and the more militant elements of many different ethnic and social groups. The city management had looked carefully for the best man available to deal with that situation; Bob McGowan had been their choice and he had given them no cause to regret it.

His reverie was interrupted when his phone rang once briefly. "Mr. Tibbs is back from court," his secretary told him. "You asked to be notified."

McGowan swung around and assumed a more businesslike posture. "Thank you. Pass the word that I'd like to see him in ten minutes. Meanwhile get Mr. Duffy on the phone for me; you can reach him at the number I gave you this morning."

While he was waiting for the call to be completed he reviewed once more a letter that had been on the top of his desk for two days; he knew perfectly well what it said, but he wanted to have it fresh in his mind before he went any further. When the phone tingled he spoke on the line for only a short time, made a commitment, and then hung up. Five minutes later the man he had sent for appeared in the doorway of his office.

Virgil Tibbs was appropriately dressed in a subdued dark suit which he frequently wore for his court appearances. His somewhat slender build suggested a quiet manner, but the parallel impression, that he was not physically very durable, was an illusion. As he came into the office a more discerning observer might have noted a suggestion of body discipline and with it a subtle air of self-possession. It was not at all evident and most people missed it entirely. Bob McGowan knew as well as anyone else that Virgil Tibbs had grown up under near-poverty conditions in the Deep South, and for a Negro boy to rise from that beginning to become the man who stood before him now had taken much more than ordinary effort and determination.

"Sit down," Bob invited.

There was no point in going through any empty preliminaries. "Virgil, I've heard from some gentlemen who would like very much to meet you, later on this afternoon if you can make it. They didn't go into too much detail with me, but I'm sure that they'll fill you in."

" 'Some gentlemen' is a little vague," Tibbs said.

Bob hadn't really expected to get away with that. "I can give you a little more," he continued. "They're

Feds and undoubtedly they want some sort of cooperation."

"If so, how far shall I commit myself?"

McGowan waved a hand casually. "I'll leave that entirely up to you; do whatever your best judgment dictates."

Tibbs contemplated him quietly for a moment. "Chief McGowan, are you sure that you don't want to give me any further instructions?"

"I wish that I could, in a way, but you'll have to take it as it is. Whatever you decide to do, I'll back you up — you can count on that."

"I'd just like some assurance that I'm not being sold down the river," Virgil said.

"Absolutely not; I wouldn't consider any such idea if there was any way to avoid it. You shouldn't have to ask that. They want to take a look at you — that's the extent of it right now."

Tibbs got to his feet. "I hope it makes them happy. When and where?"

"They're sending a car for you at three. All right with you?"

"I'll tell you when I get back," Virgil said.

He returned to his own office not overly anxious to keep the appointment that had been made for him. He had problems enough on hand, including two or three cases he was very much concerned with getting cleaned up. Business was good, unfortunately, and every man on the force was carrying a full load. The wave of terror bombings that was sweeping the country with its violence, the intransigency of the militants, the wanton murders of police officers, and the sustained international tensions in the Middle and Far East had all combined to create an atmosphere of frustration and discontent. Jobs for some time had been few and hard to find, a factor that had added even more to the sum total of irritation, actual distress, and sometimes desperation. Now the Feds wanted something and while he was sympathetic with their problems, he had plenty in stock of his own.

When the car arrived, precisely on schedule, it was a current-model Chevrolet shiny with newness. The driver was quite formal in the way he got out and held open the rear door for his passenger; it suggested that he might have been in the military and accustomed to driving the brass in the regulation manner. It also made clear that conversation was discouraged. Accepting that fact, Virgil settled down in the back seat and allowed himself to be driven away.

As the car headed north the few road noises that filtered through the closed windows and the subdued sound of the air conditioning blower were the only things that underlay the essential quiet. There being nothing else productive to do, Tibbs studied the sharply rising brown hills, baked by the strong sunlight day after day and denied water during almost all of the hot summer months. The blanket of smog that so often plagued Pasadena was heavy in the air. Behind the strongly built foothills the mountains were more massive than they appeared; the discoloration in the atmosphere made them seem almost misty even at relatively close range.

Not long after the car reached the end of the city streets it began to climb. The heat outside became more visibly evident; on either side of the road dried-out vegetation struggled to survive in the arid soil. The engine labored, pinging as it attacked the steeper grades, as though it too was suffering from the pollution in the air.

In the area toward which the driver was heading there was a number of small plants and laboratories, most of them concerned with highly advanced technology related to national defense. Almost all of them had fairly elaborate plant-protection systems which were tied in with the police network. From time to time unpublicized attempts had been made to break into these facilities; when that had happened the subsequent investigations had always been very thorough and entirely confidential. Satisfied now that he knew the general nature of his errand, Virgil allowed himself to relax and derive what enjoyment he could from the ride.

Several minutes later the car turned up a private road, and after another quarter of a mile, stopped before a set of guarded chain-link gates which gave access to what appeared to be a moderately small facility. The driver displayed a badge, the rear door was opened, and Tibbs was politely asked for his ID. He produced his police credentials and noted that they were examined rather than simply glanced at. The gates were then opened and the car was permitted to pass through.

The building itself gave very little external evidence of its purpose. It was a single-story structure built in a U shape with a small unscarred loading dock at one end and a Spanish-style tile roof unbroken except for a series of vent pipes and some restrained bits of ornamentation. Otherwise it was featureless; the only visible sign was a small one with the word RECEPTION and a directing arrow. The driver took Tibbs up to the front door and then spoke for the first time. "They'll take care of you inside," he said, and turned away.

The small, plainly furnished lobby was devoid of any of the product illustrations or civic award plaques usual in such settings. There was a switchboard operator seated behind a glass panel who barely glanced up when the door was opened; she was quite aware that there was someone in the lobby waiting to receive the visitor. A man rose to his feet as Virgil came in and moved a step or two forward. "Mr. Tibbs? My name is Duffy. Please come in; Mr. Washburn is expecting you."

He led the way by opening a substantial door that was equipped with an electric lock and then turned right down a short corridor. At the end another door gave access to the executive suite. The light green plas-

terboard walls were supplanted by dark wood paneling
and the vinyl floor tiles were replaced by heavy, foot-
inviting carpeting. Tibbs had been anticipating that his
visit would be primarily with the head of plant security; the front office environment required him to make
some rapid revisions. Before he could reach any acceptable conclusions he found himself with his guide
in the secretarial area. One of the three young women
seated there rose immediately, tapped lightly on the
door to the corner office, and then held it open for
them to go through.

The first thing that Virgil noted was the furniture,
quiet in design but of obviously superior quality. On
the large walnut desk that dominated the room there
were a few carefully chosen appointments; on a wide
windowsill behind it, a framed photograph of an unusually attractive woman with three children gathered
about her. The paneled walls were decorated with
original oil paintings of mountain scenery.

There were two men in the office waiting for them.
The one behind the desk was early middle-aged; he
had about him the aura of the health club and a well-
used swimming pool which kept his muscles toned and
his waistline in proportion. He was blond and definitely handsome, and when he held out his hand it was
built of firm flesh well accustomed to being used to do
things. "Don Washburn, Mr. Tibbs," he said as he
shook hands; then he gestured to his companion.

The second man had been sitting at one end of a

leather-covered davenport. As he came forward Virgil noted the conservative cut of the sport coat he wore and the mirror-bright shine of his shoes — they would have passed a police inspection anywhere. That was all that he needed to know for the moment. He shook hands and acknowledged the name, Lonigan; then he turned back to take his cue from the executive who was making him welcome.

"How do you take your coffee, Mr. Tibbs?" Washburn asked.

"Black, please."

The information was relayed via intercom; within a few seconds the girl opened the door once more, this time carrying four cups of coffee in imported Japanese ceramic mugs. She served them and then withdrew.

As soon as the door was closed once more, Washburn continued. "We certainly appreciate your coming up here to see us. So that you know the lay of the land, this is a research facility engaged in government work which we like to think is of considerable importance."

Virgil nodded and sipped his coffee.

"Please forgive me, Mr. Tibbs, if I don't tell you anything more about what we are doing. It is very highly classified."

"I won't mention it to anyone." Virgil promised.

"Do you know?" There was a disturbed note in Washburn's voice.

"I believe so."

"Would you mind telling me?" Politely put, it was nevertheless a demand.

"I suspect fuel research, Mr. Washburn. Probably nonhydrocarbon, but that's only a guess."

The air was heavy.

Lonigan broke the brief silence that followed. "Mr. Tibbs, excuse my bluntness, but we'd be very much interested to know how you determined that."

"For one thing, by the thickness of the carpeting." After that Virgil continued to sip his coffee.

Washburn spoke quietly. "I don't see any point in being coy about this: I'd like to know where our security slipped. I ordered the carpeting, incidentally, and if it's giving us away, please tell me how."

Virgil set down his coffee cup. "The car that picked me up was new and obviously well maintained, but when we started climbing up here the engine pinged very noticeably. Since the temperature was normal according to the gauge, that meant either a bad timing adjustment or else a low-grade fuel. I didn't think too much about it until we arrived here and I saw the number of vent pipes in your roof. That rather strongly suggested internal-combustion engines indoors, and the idea of fuel experimentation occurred to me."

"About the carpeting?"

"I was coming to that. In a very new, well-kept car it was highly unlikely that the timing adjustment would have been neglected, so I assumed that someone was trying to economize by buying cheaper gasoline. Things like that happen sometimes when a company decides to put on a drastic cost-cutting drive."

Washburn nodded. "True."

"I believe that it's clear now. This is obviously a research facility: your location and the unused condition of your loading dock made that apparent. Since air pollution by hydrocarbons is an urgent national problem, it seemed possible that you might be working on it here — and trying out your product in your own vehicles. I was still undecided in my mind until I happened to notice the carpeting, which is very new and of exceptional quality. That eliminated a stringent economy drive, so fuel research was the only good possibility that was left that I could think of."

Washburn made a note. "I'll have those vents covered up, one way or another, immediately. And we'll stop carrying passengers in our test vehicles. Anything else?"

"I believe not," Tibbs answered. "Perhaps you'd tell me now what I can do for you."

Lonigan handed over a card which read, DEPARTMENT OF JUSTICE, BUREAU OF NARCOTICS AND DANGEROUS DRUGS. Duffy also supplied one which bore the same identification. When that formality had been completed, Lonigan picked up the conversational ball.

"Mr. Tibbs, in Washington we have an unpublicized file on police officers all over the country who have special abilities. When we recently had need of a man who could speak fluent Yugoslavian, we located one promptly — he was working vice in Cleveland. Do you remember meeting a man at one time whose name was Gottschalk?"

Virgil searched his memory for a few seconds. "Yes, a missile engineer."

Lonigan nodded. "That's the one. I believe he was driving south through Wells when the local police stopped him for questioning — in connection with a murder you were looking into down there."

"Yes." Tibbs did not need to be reminded.

"He told the security people at the cape about it; he was quite impressed. That's how you first got into our files. We sent out a questionnaire on you, a confidential one of course, and a Captain Lindholm supplied us with some additional data."

Virgil showed some signs of discomfort. "I can't honestly thank him for it. He retired as assistant chief a short while ago."

Lonigan smiled. "I don't believe that he did you any harm. Now let's get down to cases if you don't mind. We are confronted by a very serious problem and we need some help; in particular we want a local officer to tie in with us. How does that sound to you?"

"Fine, if Chief McGowan approves. But I don't have any special abilities to offer. I'm not fluent in any foreign languages and I certainly don't know anything about fuel synthesis. If the problem is narcotics, we have a number of people who are very sharp, you might want to talk to them. Basically I'm a homicide man."

Apparently that created no reaction. Duffy removed a sheet of paper from his inside coat pocket and pretended to consult it. "It states here," he said, "that among other things, you hold a bona fide black belt in karate. Who gave it to you?"

"Nishiyama."

"We know Mr. Nishiyama very well; a black belt from him is harder to get than Moshe Dayan pennants in Cairo. If you went through that kind of discipline for a period of years, you must have learned a few things about the Orient along the way."

"A smattering of Japanese," Tibbs admitted, "mostly the words commonly used in training. But not very much about Japan itself other than the customs and courtesies that go with the martial arts."

"And you have also studied aikido under Takahashi."

"For about five years."

"Black belt?"

"Not yet."

Very smoothly Lonigan took charge once more. "What I'm going to tell you now may sound melodramatic, but don't take it that way — it's deadly serious."

Tibbs nodded.

"Prior to World War II the Japanese, who were in a

highly aggressive military posture at that time, systematically began to flood China with opium as a means of softening up the whole country for eventual conquest. It wasn't the first time that that device had been used. The campaign was so successful that in 1936 the Nanking Government passed legislation that required addicts to present themselves for a cure within one year or else face the death penalty. It didn't work; two years later one-eighth of all of the Chinese in Nanking itself were hopelessly hooked on narcotics. And it was steadily getting worse. It was a deliberate poisoning of a nation, and despite the enormous size and population of China, it was definitely successful."

"A little like Hitler's genocide," Virgil commented.

"Unfortunately, yes. But sixteen years later the situation was reversed. The Japanese had encouraged the growing of opium poppies and the Chinese had responded. There's a UN report that came out back in March of 1952 which established clearly that the communist Chinese were converting opium to heroin and smuggling it into Japan and the United States in quantity. And not for the profit involved. It was a deliberate attempt to weaken two potential enemies. Then, in 1969, the Republic of China supplied us with information concerning a systematic new campaign by the red Chinese to pump narcotics in increasing quantities into the United States and certain other free countries. Particular attention was given to those nations that had taken a strong anticommunist position, such as Thailand, South Korea, South Vietnam, and the Philippines."

"I understood that Thailand was an opium-producing country," Tibbs said.

"True, but the Thais don't ordinarily produce heroin, and that's what concerns us most." He paused, then walked over to one of the windows where he turned and gripped the sill with his hands as though he wanted to brace himself for what was to come next. "The war in Vietnam, and the presence of American troops there in strength, provided a ready-made opportunity to carry this policy forward. An intensive campaign was begun to get our service personnel hooked on drugs in one form or another. Large amounts of marijuana were left behind whenever the North Vietnamese or the Viet Cong abandoned an area. Other harder drugs were made easily available and all kinds of inducements were used to get our people to try them. In August 1970 Admiral William Mack admitted to a congressional committee that the drug problem within the American military in Vietnam had become a very serious matter."

Lonigan stopped again and began to walk slowly across the room. "About the most threadbare words in the American political arena are 'communist plot,' but in this instance it's quite true. And while most plots, when there are any, are by their very nature expensive, this is one which pays almost fantastic profits to its promoters."

Washburn stirred in his chair.

"You said that you're a homicide man," Duffy said. "This is mass homicide — slow death by poison. And heroin *is* poison; take a little too much and that's it."

"All right, how can I help?" Tibbs asked.

At that moment the phone on Washburn's desk rang once softly. The executive picked it up, listened, and then nodded to Virgil. "It's for you," he said.

Tibbs walked over and took the instrument. "Virgil," the voice of Bob McGowan came over the wire, "I'm calling you myself because no one else knows where you are. When you've finished, come back as soon as you can. We've got a killing and this one is far enough out to be right in your line."

CHAPTER 3

In a tight agony of desolate grief Yumeko sat very still; her eyes were closed so that she could at least partially shut out the world that surrounded her. Misery was nothing new to her; she had known it most of her life because of who and what she was, but all of the buffeting she had endured had not been sufficient to prepare her for what confronted her now. The one brief happiness she had known had been the time she had spent in Mr. Wang's house, for he was the only person who had been truly kind to her. Now it was all over, finally and completely, because Mr. Wang was dead.

And by the hand of a murderer.

This final climactic cruelty made her want very much to bring her own life to an end. She had nothing whatever to look forward to, not even the expectation of a small amount of normal happiness such as is granted to most people — for a little while at least. Because there was no one else to mourn Mr. Wang she knew that she would have to remain alive at least long enough to see that his memory was properly revered and that all of the things necessary to insure his complete happiness in the following world were attended to. After that, if she could rejoin him it would represent her dearest wish.

One of the policemen who had answered when she had called in after her terrible discovery squatted down beside her. After an awkward moment of nothingness he laid his hand on top of hers. "I'm terribly sorry, Miss Wang," he said.

His words were painful to her because she wasn't Miss Wang, but she understood that he was attempting to be kind. She opened her eyes and nodded to acknowledge his sympathy.

"I'm afraid," he continued gently, "that we won't be able to move your father for just a little while. Someone is coming — to help. After he has been here, then we'll take care of everything."

Yumeko struggled to find her voice. "Thank you."

"It won't be very long."

Yumeko had no idea how long it actually was. A blessed numbness took the sharp edge off reality, and the closed draperies before the front window shielded her from the unwanted waning sunlight. She was vaguely aware that someone else did come into Mr. Wang's house, but what had once been an event was no longer of any consequence. Again she was stabbed by the thought that she could no longer serve him and announce his callers.

Outside the rear room Virgil Tibbs listened quietly while Barry Rothberg, the uniformed officer who had first answered the summons, filled him in. "We got the call just under an hour ago. Apparently there were only two people living here, the victim and his daughter, who discovered the body. She's still here. Badly shocked, I'd say — no one's tried to question her yet."

"Any other witnesses?"

Rothberg shook his head. "None that we know of. Chief McGowan himself passed the word that nothing was to be disturbed until you got here. By which I take it that this one is all yours."

"It looks that way," Virgil said. Then he entered the room where the dead man lay on the floor. Calmly, and quite deliberately, he first looked around him at the display cabinets filled with their rare treasures, then at the thick, tightly closed draperies which entirely blocked out the windows. He noted the rich red carpeting and then, the preliminaries over, he gave his full attention to Mr. Wang as he lay in death in the midst of what had been his cherished possessions.

Before he came any closer to the body, Tibbs knelt down and with the palm of his hand tested the ability of the carpeting to hold any kind of a footprint. His finding was negative; the pile was of a weave that would betray nothing. That determined he took a step or two forward and carefully studied the bizarre sight before him.

Mr. Wang lay on his back with his hands at his sides as though he had assumed that position voluntarily. His face, while vacant, was almost serene; even his unflinching eyes appeared to be fixed on something of their own choosing. In the center of the room there was a small sturdy table which was draped with a piece of black velvet; a tiny spotlight set in the ceiling directed a pencil of light down toward its center. Between the table and the display cases on the right-hand side of the room the body of Mr. Wang rested at an angle of approximately thirty degrees to the wall. Two of the jade cabinets were open, although they gave no external evidence of having been forced. Their contents were only slightly disturbed. From their resting places on the glass shelves four of the jades had been removed and placed on the floor; they sat in a rough semicircle, two on each side of the head of their late owner. One more piece of jade had also been taken from its display position; the *Ya-Chang* ritual knife protruded obscenely, and with deadly finality, from the left-hand side of Mr. Wang's chest.

Virgil studied the scene for some time, standing quietly still in one spot, his right hand slowly massaging the underside of his chin. When he had satisfied himself he bent over the body where it lay on the floor and studied it carefully. Behind him Agent Floyd

Sanderson waited patiently; he had seen Virgil work before and he knew enough not to interfere.

"What did the doctor say?" Tibbs asked.

"Not a great deal; he pronounced him dead and fixed the time of death as of about four or five hours ago."

Virgil took hold of one lifeless hand and flexed the arm slightly. Then he asked another question without looking up. "Has the air conditioning been on?"

"I'm not sure, Virg," Sanderson answered. "Perhaps the girl can tell you. From the feel of things when we arrived here, I'd guess not."

Tibbs nodded. "I think you're right; it's quite warm in here."

He continued his inspection of the body of the dead man, dropping down on his knees to do so, but being very careful in his movements not to disturb the jades that had been placed on the rug. "How about pictures?" he asked.

"Already taken, both black-and-white and color. No prints yet, though — he's on his way."

"Good. He may be here a while. These pieces could have been chosen at random, in which case others may have been handled too. Do you see any reason for this kind of a display?"

Sanderson shook his head. "It beats me; I've never encountered anything like it before."

"Neither have I, except in the second act of *Tosca*. I have a suspicion that there may be a lot more here than is visible right now. Two or three things don't fit."

"Such as?"

Tibbs got back to his feet. "I'm not sure of anything yet. Give me time."

He turned as the fingerprint man came into the room. "I don't envy you this job," Virgil said, then looked around him. "There must be close to a hundred and fifty pieces in those cabinets."

The fingerprint expert set his kit down on the small center table. "You want me to do them all, Virg?" he asked.

Tibbs reconsidered. "Why don't you examine the pieces in the unlocked cabinets. Leave the locked ones as they are. Later on, if there's a need, you can check the others."

"Good idea." Opening his kit the identification specialist prepared to go to work. He laid out some camel's hair brushes, several bottles of assorted kinds of black powder, and rolls of extra-wide Cellophane tape.

Satisfied that for the moment there was nothing more for him to do in the room, Virgil looked again at Sanderson. "You mentioned a girl," he said.

The sergeant gestured. "His daughter, I believe. She's in the front parlor. One of the boys tried to talk to her, but she was up pretty tight."

Virgil nodded. "I'll see what I can do. Keep things under control, will you?" He turned and reentered what was the dining room. It was done in excellent taste; the furniture had about it a casual suggestion of the Orient but it was subdued so that the beauty of the teakwood had a full opportunity to reveal itself. Tibbs ran his hand over the back of one of the chairs and confirmed the fine workmanship. Mr. Wang had not been a man who had sacrificed everything else to expand and develop his jade collection; clearly he had been a person of substantial means and with a fine appreciation of the good things of life.

The draperies hung at the windows were partly open, but their weight and texture again gave evidence of Mr. Wang's obvious love of privacy. Chinese were a rarity in this section of Pasadena and it was a possibility that Mr. Wang had preferred to keep his presence as inostentatious as possible. Under the window there was an aquarium in which a number of exotic fish swam lazily about. The whole atmosphere of the room was one of tranquillity, a place where food could have been consumed to the accompaniment of enlightened and even brilliant conversation. At that moment Tibbs wished that he might have had the privilege of dining with Mr. Wang. It would have been an event.

That conclusion reached and disposed of, he walked quietly across the fine carpeting and entered the living room.

The girl who sat there looked up at him as he came in, but with eyes which had been dulled by shock and pain. After perhaps a second they changed and a certain hardness appeared, a hostility which was not necessarily directed against him, but perhaps at what he stood for and represented. He did not understand it until he looked a little more closely at the girl herself. Then he knew that she was not the daughter of Mr. Wang.

Without waiting to be asked to do so he sat down, choosing a chair close enough to talk comfortably with the girl, but not so close that he intruded either on her privacy or her grief. When he spoke, his voice was quiet, human, and considerate. "I am terribly sorry to have to disturb you at a time like this."

It took the girl a few seconds to react to his words; he understood this and waited. Then she answered him. "It is all right."

Virgil studied her without appearing to do so. "I know that Mr. Wang was your very dear friend. May I ask your name?"

The girl came to life enough to brush her black hair away from her face. "My name is Yumeko Nagashima." It was left as a simple statement of fact.

"You are Japanese, then."

She looked at him steadily, almost reproachfully, for a long moment. "You know what I am," she said. "You have eyes and you should know. I am *ainoko*."

Tibbs did not know that word, but he was fairly sure that he could guess its meaning. "You were born in Japan?"

"Yes."

"How long ago?"

She answered the question without feeling. "I have twenty-six years."

"Are you married?

"No."

"May I call you Yumeko?"

"If it is your wish."

"Where did you learn English, Yumeko?"

"In school. In Japan."

"Your English is excellent. My Japanese is limited to just a few words."

"It is not necessary that you learn." There was a tinge of contempt in that, only a very slight hint, but Virgil caught it and it shaped his next question.

"Are you a teacher?"

"No."

He relaxed deliberately and shifted his tack a little. "My karate sensei tells me that I should learn Japanese."

"You are *karateka*?" That was what he wanted, some initiative from her, no matter how limited.

"Shodan desu," he said. That was a measurable percentage of his total Japanese vocabulary.

Her eyes widened slightly at that and the dullness receded a little. "You are black belt?"

"Yes."

"You have certificate from Japan?"

"Yes."

That halted things while she studied the man who sat near her and reevaluated him in the light of her new knowledge. "You are policeman?" she asked finally. It was a rhetorical question which provided another opening.

"Yes, I am. Yumeko, what does *ainoko* mean?"

She let her head dip until she was looking at her fingers in her lap. "It is translated 'love child.' My mother and my father did not become married. He was a U.S. GI." She looked up and met his eyes fully. "His name I do not know; my mother would never tell me. But he was a black man — like you."

Tibbs looked at her and read again the story of her ancestry. Her eyes were unmistakably Oriental, her nose slightly flattened, her skin dark enough to be clearly Negroid. And he knew without being told the hell that her life so far had been. He at least was a member of a specific group. The whites had largely despised him in the Deep South, but amongst his own fellows he had found companionship and full equality. This girl, he knew, would be rejected by the Japanese, and the sensitive Negro community would have none of her. She was Japanese and she was not; she was Negro and she was not. Only in such places as Jamaica, Brazil, or possibly Hawaii would she be likely to find others like herself or else full disregard of her mixed origin.

Yumeko began to speak again, almost as if she were doing penance. "My mother was a lovely lady; she was married and had two sons — my half brothers. Then in the war her husband was killed. When it was over and the GIs came, we were starving. She could find no work, for she was a housewife, not a business person. But because she was beautiful, many Americans wanted to shack up with her. She did this so that my brothers could have food and a place to live. Later, when I was born, my father had already leaved. He did not know."

"Your mother is in Japan now?"

Yumeko shook her head with finality. Virgil guessed at the truth and diverted her to another topic. "Mr. Wang was your benefactor?" he asked.

The girl swallowed hard and then forced herself to reply. "He was my life," she said simply. "For a little time he gave me happiness. I would do anything for him — anything."

Tibbs understood that in the way that it was meant. "Did he bring you to this country?"

Yumeko nodded. "I was of small service to him when he was in Japan. He wished an interpreter and he was willing to accept me. When he found out — the conditions of my life — he made offer to me to come and keep his house for him. As you say, without strings. Within the months that I was here with him I found for the first time what it is to be happy." Quite simply, without preliminaries, she broke down into silent tears.

Virgil waited until she began to recover, then, silently, he handed her a clean handkerchief. She took it and wiped her eyes. There had been times when others had refused that accommodation from him. "Do you have any other friends here?" he asked.

Yumeko answered by shaking her head.

"I believe that I can arrange for someone to look after you."

Again the girl shook her head; then she spoke. "I will care for myself," she said.

"You can be comfortable here?"

"Yes."

"Then in that case I would like to ask you not to leave until we know a little more than we do now. We may need you to help us." He put it that way in order to give her something to hang onto; to provide a bit of moral support. When her first surge of grief passed, she might well become completely unstrung.

"Before I go, Yumeko, may I ask just a few more questions?"

She nodded.

"Mr. Wang was, I take it, a man of considerable wealth."

"I do not know."

"Let me put it this way: did Mr. Wang have any business activities that you know of?"

"Yes," she said. "He sold jade."

That cast a new light on the matter. "Then all of the pieces that I saw were not his private collection — they were his stock in trade — is that right?"

Yumeko composed herself and tried to sit a little straighter in her chair. "Mr. Wang sold jade and he received visitors here who wished to buy. But not all of the pieces were for sale. Some he would sell, others were his own — treasures. Sometimes people came just to look. He would allow this, when he knew the person who asked."

"Mr. Wang was an authority on jade, I take it."

"Yes, he was very very wise. And very honest. When he receive a carving that was false jade, he would not sell it. Once when a man wanted one very much, Mr. Wang said that he sold only genuine stones and gave it to him instead. And he was a rich man who came to buy."

"When was this, Yumeko?"

"It was yesterday."

Tibbs took out his notebook. "Do you remember the name of the man?" he asked.

Once more she nodded. "Yes, it was Mr. Donald Washburn."

CHAPTER 4

Don Washburn himself held open the front door of his palatial home to welcome Virgil Tibbs inside. If he was in any way annoyed by the early evening call he concealed it completely. Nor was his greeting overly effusive; he was cordial to precisely the right degree. He led the way through a very long and expensively furnished living room to an enclosed porch at the rear of the house. There he motioned toward a chair while he stepped behind an elaborate small bar. "What will it be?" he asked.

"Do you have Cherry Heering?"

"Certainly: on the rocks or straight up?"

"On the rocks."

Washburn nodded. "Good man." He poured two drinks into fine glassware and served his guest with one of them. Then he dropped into a chair and faced Tibbs at a slight angle which implied sociability. "What can I do for you?" he asked.

Virgil sampled his drink carefully and then adjusted the tone of his voice before he replied. "Mr. Washburn, how well did you know Mr. Wang Fu-sen?"

His host reacted to that at once. "I don't understand your use of the past tense."

"I regret very much to bring you this news," Tibbs said, "but Mr. Wang is dead. He passed away early this afternoon."

"Naturally?" Washburn was sharp, there was no doubt about that.

"No, sir, he was murdered."

"Good God!"

Virgil sat quietly and let Washburn take his time. The big, handsome, blond man gave every appearance of being genuinely shocked by the news. When he had recovered himself he spoke again, "Can you tell me any more about it?"

"Not a great deal. He was killed, apparently without too much of a struggle, and left lying on the floor of the room where he kept his jade. I mean no implications by this, but I understand that you were one of his last visitors."

Slowly Washburn nodded. "I saw him yesterday," he acknowledged. "I called on him at his home. It was essentially a business call, but I have known Mr. Wang for some time and our relationship had become a quite personal one. That should answer your opening question, by the way." He stopped and took solace in his drink.

"Are you a jade collector, Mr. Washburn?"

In a calm and quiet voice his host answered. "Yes, to a modest degree. I would like to think of myself as a student of jade and jade carving. It is a vast and intricate culture of its own, Mr. Tibbs, and to my mind one of the most fascinating subjects in the world."

"Would you describe Mr. Wang as an authority?"

"Absolutely, there's no question about that. And, I might add, he is, or was, one of the most honest men it would be possible to imagine. I can give proof of that."

"You were a customer of his, I take it?"

Again Washburn nodded. "Yes, I would say that Mr. Wang sold me about seventy percent of my collection, as a guess. Not that it is extensive; actually he encouraged me to buy fewer pieces and to concentrate on very good ones. They are more rewarding to own and they appreciate faster. Very fine work, for the most part, isn't being done anymore."

"How did you acquire the other thirty percent?"

"From various sources. Gumps in San Francisco, one or two pieces I bought in Taipei — they have very fine jade there if you know where to go. Not the tourist stuff, but the real *chen yu* — true jade."

"There are imitations, then?"

Washburn waved a hand. "Gosh, yes — multitudes, and most of it is passed off as the real thing, of course. They call it by a variety of names — new jade, Soo Chow jade, soft jade — but none of them are real jade."

"I believe that you're underrating your own knowledge," Tibbs said. "Obviously you know what you're talking about."

"Superficially, perhaps, but compared to real experts like Mr. Wang or Goh Keng Tong I can't even sit on the bench."

Tibbs shifted in his chair. "This afternoon," he said, "I had the pleasure of meeting you under very different circumstances. Right now I am engaged in the case of Mr. Wang's death, which will probably prevent me from taking part in any antinarcotics activity until the matter is resolved. My new role makes it necessary for me to ask you some additional questions."

"Certainly. Should I have my lawyer present?"

Virgil finished his drink and answered while his host was preparing him another. "If you so desire, then by all means call him. However, at the present time I'm interested principally in background information which doesn't concern you personally."

Washburn brought the fresh drinks over and resumed his seat. "That's a relief, and I'm sure we understand each other on that point. You see, I've heard of you too."

Tibbs did understand, and he let the matter rest there. "You are the head of the company I visited this afternoon?"

"Yes, Washburn Associates. The name is deliberately noncommital."

"Do you do other work besides fuel research?"

"Yes, but those activities are strictly classified. If

you need to know about them, you will have to clear the appropriate security people first. If they give me the green light, then I'll be glad to brief you fully."

"I don't think that will be necessary if you can answer one question for me now," Virgil said. "Are dangerous drugs — in the sense of dangerous for human use without medical direction — in any way involved?"

Washburn threw his head back and thought. It took him several seconds to make up his mind. "I *will* answer that, since in a way the information has already been compromised and you would have to be told anyway. This is absolutely confidential: we are working for and with the Bureau of Narcotics and Dangerous Drugs. Chemistry is our bag; for reasons that I would rather not go into right now, we are in a position to do the work we are doing for the Bureau."

"Would these facts account for my meeting Duffy and Lonigan at your plant rather than at their own offices?"

Washburn was very slightly uncomfortable with that question, but he answered it. "To a degree, certainly. Perhaps I'd better add a little to that. I have a personal interest in the work of the Bureau which goes beyond our professional association. I have what you might call a hobby interest in young people."

Tibbs waited a moment before he spoke again. "Mr. Washburn, by any chance do you have four children?"

His host looked at him keenly. "You know, then?"

Virgil shook his head. "It was a surmise, that's all. I saw the family picture in your office with the three young children, but you could well be the father of a teen-ager."

Don Washburn did not hesitate. "I have a seventeen-year-old son, Mr. Tibbs. Without discounting our love for our other children, Robin has always been very close to us. He was born with a clubfoot which, thank God, was fully corrected — you'd never know it now. When he was fifteen, Mr. Tibbs — *fifteen*, mind you — some beast of a peddler got him to sniff a fine white powder without knowing what it was."

"Heroin?"

Washburn was grim. "Yes. I was not aware of what had happened until early summer when, unaccountably, he refused to use the pool. Up until then swimming had been a big thing with him: he could hardly wait for the start of the season. I'll spare you the details; we found out what it was and why he was afraid to let us see his forearms. I took him to our doctor. He filed a report as he was required to do, and shortly after that your narcotics people contacted me. Eventually I met Mr. Duffy and following a check that he made, I was given an opportunity to strike back."

"I understand," Virgil said. "And, believe me, I sympathize. Where is your son now?"

"In Kentucky."

"Lexington?"

"Yes."

Tibbs rose. "One more thing before I go. Do you by any chance know any of Mr. Wang's other friends or associates? Or any potential enemies?"

"There's a man named Johnny Wu in Chinatown. I haven't met him, but I understand that he too is a jade dealer. Quite a different type of individual, but that doesn't imply any lack of integrity."

"And the girl?"

Washburn shook his head. "A mystery to me. I was introduced to her and found her very ladylike, but I do not understand her to any degree. I gather that in some way Mr. Wang was her benefactor, but I don't know any details. I doubt if the obvious thing is true; he simply wasn't that kind of a man. One who would take advantage of homeless girls, I mean."

"Thank you very much, Mr. Washburn."

Five minutes later Virgil was outside, looking up into the clear evening sky as though he could read directions there. He got back into his car and consulted his watch. The temptation to go home was strong; he had already had an overlong day and the court grilling in the morning had gotten it off to anything but a good start. On the other hand the Los Angeles Chinatown scarcely stirred before midafternoon and if he wanted to see Johnny Wu, the time would never be better than the present.

He started the engine and began to drive toward the entrance to the Pasadena Freeway. It was old and twisting, but it would take him into the heart of the city in a few minutes and he did not even need to go that far; the Chinatown area lay close to the super-highway a mile or two short of the four-level inter-change.

He rolled down the window to take advantage of the breeze that would be generated as soon as he picked up to the allowable fifty-five miles an hour on his way into the city. The unmarked police car he was driving was equipped with the standard model four-seventy air conditioning: roll down all four windows and then drive seventy miles an hour. He thought again about the silent figure lying at an angle in the middle of the floor with the ancient jade knife all but buried in the heart. And surrounding it, the four other jade carvings placed in a grisly watch. He thought about all five of the pieces of jade and asked himself many questions.

He was so intent in his thought processes that he nearly missed his turnoff. He left the freeway by means of what he knew to be an illegal lane change and was grateful that no one saw him do it, no one, at least, who was in a position to take any official action. Free of that potential embarrassment he maneuvered through the short, up-and-down streets of the near north side until he broke out on North Broadway. Three minutes later he pulled into the parking lot opposite the ornate entranceway to New Chinatown, an investment by the local merchants which had paid bountiful dividends. He slipped the plain tan-colored car into a slot, locked it, and held out his hand to the young Mexican attendant for the ticket. He received only a silent shake of the head and then was waved away.

How he had recognized his vehicle Tibbs did not know, but he was in no mood to debate the point. He crossed the street and walked past the statue of Sun Yat-sen which occupied the place of honor in the entrance court. Then he was surrounded by the closely packed restaurants, souvenir shops, and novelty houses which stocked everything from gaudy trash to a limited number of genuinely fine items. Virgil walked into a store at random and spoke to the short, stocky Chinese woman who was closest to him behind the counter. "Where can I find Johnny Wu?" he asked.

The woman evaluated him with a single look that missed very little. "Is he expecting you?" she asked.

Tibbs shook his head. "I'm a police officer," he said. "I'd like to talk to him."

"He might be at General Lee's."

"Thank you very much."

He walked up the street a few doors to the entrance to one of the largest and most popular restaurants in the area. Almost at once a slender Chinese beauty in a green sheath greeted him. "Good evening, sir. Dinner for one?"

Virgil smiled at her; he would have done that if he had been dying. "I'm looking for Mr. Johnny Wu. Is he here by any chance?"

The girl studied him for a moment. "I'll find out, sir," she said.

"Thank you. Please tell him that Mr. Tibbs would like to speak with him if it's convenient."

He waited a short while, taking in the scene at the bar which was so like so many tens of thousands of others. Bars, he decided, had a uniformity about them that exceeded almost any other form of enterprise. This one was in a Chinese restaurant, but the drinks being served up were essentially the same as they would have been anywhere else. He was considering the value of a man's drinking habits as a means of identification when the girl returned. "If you will come with me, Mr. Tibbs?" She made it a question, then turned and led him up the staircase which hugged the right wall.

The second floor was an expanse of dining areas which had been carefully designed to suggest that they were separate entities. As Virgil looked about he realized once more how times had changed for the better. He could remember when a Chinese restaurant was a place where white people went to eat chop suey and perhaps inhale a small portion of exotic atmosphere. Most of them had offered a minimum of decor and based their appeal on meals that cost a little less. General Lee's hardly fitted that mold. Despite the late hour it was well filled with diners, Asians and Occidentals who ate together or separately, and distinguishable only by the slight difference in their features. When he noted a Negro couple quietly enjoying themselves, he was grateful for the fact that this was a new generation, not in age, but in thought.

The girl ahead of him walked with easy grace as she led him to a small alcove where, at a table that normally would have been reserved for at least four, a single man was seated. She nodded her head slightly to Tibbs, eyed him for a fraction of a second, and then silently withdrew.

"Sit down, Mr. Tibbs," the man said. "You look like you could use a drink."

Compared to the still form of Mr. Wang, Johnny Wu was a complete antithesis. He appeared to be of medium height, slightly rotund, and somewhere in early middle age. His Chinese ancestry could be read in his face, but that was as far as it went in his external deportment. He stood up to shake hands formally, then sat down again and without waiting for a comment from Tibbs signaled for a waiter. One was at his elbow almost immediately. "What will relieve your anguish?" he asked.

"What are you having?"

The waiter understood and left. As Tibbs sat down, Wu took the initiative. "You've come to see me about the death of Wang Fu-sen, I believe. I hope that you'll apply all your talents to finding whoever it was that did him in."

"You know then," Virgil said.

"Of course, things like that don't remain hidden.

Especially when a man of Wang's stature is involved, and when it's on the newscasts."

"I see." He hadn't known that the murder had been made public that quickly. "It would be a real help if you'd tell me all you can about him. Particularly any enemies he might have had."

Johnny Wu picked up a piece of paper-wrapped chicken and unfolded it. "You're *Virgil* Tibbs, aren't you?"

"Yes, that's right."

"Didn't you work on a murder done in a nudist camp?"

"True."

"Lots of pretty girls running around with no clothes on."

"Some."

"Charlie Chan never got a break like that."

Virgil kept his face unchanged. "He had a large family," he answered. "He didn't need it."

Wu considered that. "You have a point," he conceded. "But don't say 'had.' Charlie is still living. He's an old man, of course, retired in Honolulu. I've met him."

"Indeed," Tibbs said. The two men looked at each other, then Virgil spoke again. "Since Mr. Chan is in retirement, I don't presume that I can consult him."

"Probably not. He is devoting himself to a study of ancient systems of calligraphy."

"In that case, perhaps you will help me. Do you know who did in Mr. Wang?"

Johnny Wu became serious. "No, I do not." He paused while Virgil's drink was served. "He mentioned to me once that some sort of difficulty had arisen, but he was the kind of person who might have said that very casually — it was impossible to tell."

"Do you think that it might have involved his houseguest?"

"Yumeko? I doubt it. She's all right, I think. She's not a happy person, but I'd bet that she thought the world of Fu-sen. He was a genuine humanitarian."

"I understand that you also deal in jade, Mr. Wu."

"Johnny, please — I don't like formality. I do some jade dealing, yes, but right now there isn't too much to work with. I don't want any of Chairman Mao's junk — and that's what most of it is — and the supply of good merchandise is way off. Occasionally something comes in, but not often enough to make it a profitable line. Consequently I haven't gone out for business in jade to any degree. I fill a few orders now and then when I'm lucky."

Tibbs thought about that, then tried out his drink. He couldn't name it or its ingredients, but it was excellent. "Did Mr. Wang have the same difficulties in getting good merchandise?" he asked.

Johnny Wu shook his head. "I'd say that he had the best sources of anyone in the country. He seemed to be able to find excellent pieces when nobody else could. I've been on the other side several times on business and once I tried hard to develop some legitimate sources, but I didn't really get anywhere. Lots of imitation stuff was available, but nobody who knows anything wants that. There was some new work that had come out of Peking by various routes, but it was all fourth- or fifth-rate at the best. Nothing to compare with what was done during the Ching Dynasty. Do you know your Chinese history?"

"No," Tibbs admitted.

"You ought to brush up a little. And read a couple of good books on jade. You're a cultured man; you should know something about it. If you're going to find out who killed Wang Fu-sen, you'd better know about jade."

"In your opinion, then, his death may be connected with jade in some way?"

"Well, since he was stabbed to death with a jade knife, which I suspect was probably not a knife at all, I would definitely say so, yes."

Tibbs looked at his fingers for a moment, then he studied the face of the man opposite him. "Your point is well taken," he said, "but there is one detail. I don't know it for a fact yet, but I'm almost certain that the knife I saw sticking out of his chest didn't kill him at all."

CHAPTER 5

After he had enjoyed a good night's rest, Virgil Tibbs felt much more ready to take on the problems of the world in general and those connected with the death of Wang Fu-sen in particular. At the same time he wished a little fervently that people could learn to behave themselves. They set up laws of their own making and then seemed determined to break them all on a systematic basis. Sometimes it was nothing more than pushing the speed limit a few miles per hour, but it also included the elimination of an unwanted person by cold and permanent murder.

From his office he phoned up to Chief McGowan to tell him that the murder of the Chinese jade merchant looked like a sticky one, bad enough that he could not see his way clear to extend much cooperation to the Bureau of Narcotics and Dangerous Drugs until it had been cleaned up. Bob McGowan understood and promised to pass the word on to the federal authorities.

When that had been done, Bob Nakamura, his office mate who had been patiently waiting to get in a word of his own, had news. "The jury is back," he reported. "You've got a conviction."

Tibbs was grimly satisfied. "On the third try. Is he going to the joint?"

"Five years, I'd guess."

"I just hope now that he doesn't get out again in eighteen months on parole. There are still too many little girls in this town who don't always have adult protection."

"I know," Nakamura said. "Another thing: the preliminary print report on the Chinese murder — nothing. The victim himself and a young woman who is living in the house showed up — that's all. Incidentally, I understand that she's Japanese."

"Yes, but she doesn't know it," Tibbs answered. "She gave me the word for it. Her father was a Negro GI."

"Was it *ainoko*?"

"That sounds right."

The bespectacled, crew-cut, Babbitt-looking Nisei detective turned around in his chair to face his partner. "Virg, she belongs to a group that's had it exceptionally tough. Most of the Japanese will reject her completely. You can judge how far she would be welcomed into the Negro community."

Virgil shook his head. "Not very far," he conceded. "Same old story; she's too different."

"Exactly. For her there's no easy place to go, because nobody really wants her."

Tibbs picked up a pencil and studied it as he spoke. "I've only seen her once, and at a bad time for her, but she impressed me as having some pretty fair assets."

"Could you call her attractive?"

"Why not." He put down the pencil. "As a person, mind you. She was pretty damn unhappy when I interviewed her, but under different circumstances she might have considerable appeal. Admittedly I wasn't considering her particularly in that light when we were talking."

"How about it?" Nakamura asked. "Was she playing concubine to the late lamented?"

Virgil picked up the pencil once more and then tossed it down. "I'll cover a bet against that," he said firmly. "It just wasn't in the atmosphere. And the deceased was an old man. I know that can be a fooler, but I still won't buy it."

"Anything I can do to help?"

Tibbs stood up. "Yes, call the morgue and make sure that the cause of death isn't presumed too readily because of the stone knife that was in the decedent's chest. Incidentally, I suspect that it's quite valuable in addition to being important evidence."

He did some hard thinking as he drove his official car through the familiar streets to his destination. He did not propose to take up the study of jade, but he did not like to feel that his ignorance of the subject might prove to be a handicap. He decided to get hold of one good book on the subject and read it just in case. While jade collecting did not go with a policeman's salary, an understanding of that exotic subject could be rewarding in itself.

As he pulled up outside the still carefully shuttered house he expected that Yumeko would be there, but he was not sure exactly what he was going to say to her. When he rang the bell she answered almost immediately and held the door open for him to come in. "Good morning, Mr. Tibbs," she said.

"Good morning, Miss Nagashima."

"It is Yumeko," she said very simply.

He smiled at her. "Then in that case it's Virgil."

He followed her into the house and sat down on invitation in the same room that they had occupied before. "Are you feeling any better now?" he asked.

She nodded. "Yes, I thank you. My employer, Mr. Tanaka, was very kind. He has excused me after only one day to be here."

"Are you sure that you're all right, and will be after we have finished here?"

"Yes."

He waited for more, but she had nothing to add.

"Yumeko, it is my job to find out who killed Mr. Wang. Would you like to see me succeed?"

She lifted her head a little and looked at him. "Yes, very much."

"Then I want you to answer some questions for me — even if it's hard. There are many things I have to know."

"Please ask."

He tried to make his voice sympathetic without being sticky about it. "Let's begin with Mr. Wang's relatives. Did he have any in this country that you know of?"

She shook her head. "He said once to me that he was alone here. He had a younger brother, but he is in communist China. If he is still alive. Mr. Wang did not know."

"Was he married at any time?"

"I only know that he spoke of his daughter once. In this country that would make him have a wife also. In China perhaps not."

"I understand. Do you know where she is?"

"Also in China, I think. He did not say for sure."

"All of the jade in this house, it was his?"

"Yes, all his."

"It must be worth a fortune."

"I think yes."

"Yumeko, did he ever speak to you about a will?"

This time she shook her head and remained silent.

"Then as far as you know, Mr. Wang had no living relatives in this country or in any other part of the free world."

"That is yes," she answered.

"Do you know if he had an attorney?"

"Yes, Mr. Finegold. He is also a buyer of the jade."

"Yumeko, was jade-selling Mr. Wang's full-time occupation?"

He saw confusion on her face and tried to put it another way. "Did he do any other work? Or did he have enough money to meet his needs? Do you know?"

The girl looked at him a little strangely for a moment. "It is the jade-selling that was his work," she answered. "He also was not poor, but it was the jade that he loved."

"Did many customers come to see him?"

"A few. Much he sold by mail. He would send pictures and the people trusted him. He would then mail the jade if they bought it. If pieces were very valuable, he would sometimes make a messenger."

"Is there a file of Mr. Wang's customers?"

"Yes, of course. I kept it for him while I was here."

Then, visibly, she seemed to think of something. She looked quickly at the ceiling for a moment, then back at Tibbs. "I made a mistake," she said. "The jade here, it was not all Mr. Wang's. One piece was not his; he had selled it to Mr. Harvey. When the TV said that Mr. Wang was dead, Mr. Harvey called me very soon: he now wants his jade."

Virgil weighed that. Harvey's action, whoever he was, had been inconsiderate, but if he had paid a substantial price, then he had a right to protect his investment and his purchase. "Where does Mr. Harvey live?" he asked.

Yumeko raised a hand and brushed her midnight-black hair back from her deep-toned face. "It is a place called Sierra Madre."

"Would you like me to deliver the jade to him?"

For the first time since they had met he saw animation in her features. "You would do this for me?"

"Of course." He saw no need to explain that he wanted to interview some more of Mr. Wang's nearby customers and that this provided him with a very convenient opportunity.

Yumeko got up. "Come, please," she said. "I will prepare it in its box."

"I'll give you a receipt for it," Tibbs volunteered. "And I'll get one from Mr. Harvey. It may be important for you to have it."

She did not reply to that; instead she led the way toward the back of the house. Unconsciously he compared her walk to that of the Chinese girl who had ushered him into General Lee's to see Johnny Wu. Yumeko was graceful, but in a quite different way. The Chinese girl had been an inch and a half taller and definitely more slender. Yumeko was very well proportioned, but with a slight fullness in the bosom and a trace in the hips which could be attributed to her father's genes.

At the door to the jade room she hesitated for a scant moment before she pressed the light switch and then passed inside. The body had been removed and the pieces of jade which had been standing around it on the carpeting had been picked up and placed together back in the display case from which they had been taken. But on the rich red of the velvet-pile carpeting there was a chalk outline which conjured up with too vivid imagery the still, silent figure that had lain there the day before.

Carefully avoiding that spot, Yumeko opened the bottom section of one of the cabinets and reached inside. After some groping she produced a small packet of keys. As she stood up, she explained. "Mr. Wang always he kept the keys to the jade cabinets, but there was this extra set if it became necessary."

She unlocked the glass door of one of the cabinets on the left side of the room and with cautious care removed a pale green figure of a standing Chinese beauty. The eight-inch-high statuette held a tray on which were displayed several pieces of miniature fruit. A slight discoloration in the original stone had been cunningly utilized by the sculptor to make one of the fruit pieces different from the rest, a reddish yellow contrast which accentuated the whole work. As Yumeko stood it in the middle of the center table, the tiny concealed spotlight in the ceiling illuminated it in a way that almost made it come to life.

Tibbs did not want even to touch it, but as he bent down to examine it more closely the exquisite craftsmanship fascinated him. It had a delicate, subtle grace which seemed to deny the possibility that it had been carved out of a single hard, cold piece of a rare and costly stone. At that moment the prospect of learning a little about jade became much more appealing. He knew that the piece before him must be very expensive, but he was unable even to guess at its dollar value.

From under the display portion of the cabinet Yumeko took out a small stack of blue cloth-covered boxes and began to sort them on the floor. She quickly found the one she wanted and replaced the others. Placing it on the table, she opened it to reveal its carefully padded, satin-lined interior and lovingly placed the jade figurine on the preformed cushion. It fitted precisely into the indentation that had been prepared for it. The little carved wooden stand nested in its own prepared slot at the bottom. Against the snow-white cloth the jade beauty seemed more exquisite than ever.

"Does each jade have its own special box?" Tibbs asked.

"Yes — almost always." Yumeko closed the lid and slipped the ivory pins into position. "If you will give this into the hands of Mr. Harvey," she said. "You will do Mr. Wang and me a great kindness. I will give you the address."

As she went to get it for him, Virgil carefully wrote in his notebook and then tore out the page. When Yumeko returned he handed her his receipt for the valuable jade. "That was not necessary," she said. "I honor your face."

Tibbs shook his head. "We must be especially careful now," he told her. "I'll get a receipt from Mr. Harvey. It's the only proper way when valuable property is involved."

She accepted that. "You will come back?" she asked.

Virgil glanced at her for a moment, but it had been a simple inquiry and nothing more. "Yes, I'll be back." He took the address from her, memorized it, and then put the slip of paper into his pocket. That done, he picked up the jade box, and carrying it carefully, went out to his car.

A little under a half hour later he pressed the doorbell belonging to a residence clearly in one of the highest categories that Sierra Madre had to offer. Ordinarily he would have made an appointment; this time he was doing things a little differently. In Yumeko's references to Mr. Harvey he had detected a hesitant note; he wanted to know why it had been there.

The man who answered his ring came close to supplying an answer by his appearance alone. He was an inch over six feet tall, and quite lean. His presence in the doorway was like a cold wind. "Yes?" he asked.

"Mr. Harvey?"

The door was beginning to close slightly when Tibbs detected a change; the man confronting him glanced down for the first time and saw the box in his hands. The door swung wider. "Come in," he said, but there was no invitation in his voice — only a basic command.

Virgil walked into the foyer and confirmed that the interior of the house was as splendidly furnished as the exterior had suggested. A rich, thick white carpeting covered a vast area of living room and extended around one open end into another room. In another day it could have been a morning room, but the end of a billiards table was visible and also part of an elaborate bar.

"I'll take it," Harvey said, and did so literally before Tibbs could hand the box over. He put it on a small table, opened it, and then examined the stone carving for a few seconds in uninterrupted silence. Then he put it back almost carelessly into its box. "Thank you," he said. "You can go."

"I'd like to speak to you for a few minutes if I may," Tibbs said.

Harvey was curt. "I'm sorry, I never give out information on the market."

"I was not about to ask for any."

"I make no donations."

"Not interested," Tibbs said.

"And most emphatically I do not subscribe to magazines at the door."

"Nor do I."

"Then precisely who are you?"

"A police officer, Mr. Harvey. I brought out your

jade as a favor to Miss Nagashima. Now may we talk for a little while?"

The pronounced chill was still in the air. "You have credentials?"

"Certainly." As he preferred to do, Virgil produced a calling card. His reluctant host looked at it and then spoke. "We are not in Pasadena now."

"I'm quite aware of that, sir," Tibbs answered dryly. He did not elaborate.

"Very well, then." Harvey led the way to the nearest place where they could both sit and indicated by the way that he adjusted himself that he expected the interview to be a brief one.

It was Virgil's ball and he picked it up. "Mr. Harvey, I am the officer assigned to investigate the death of Mr. Wang, the gentleman from whom you purchased the jade I just delivered. I believe you are aware that he lost his life under somewhat unusual circumstances?"

"According to the news reports, he was stabbed to death with a stone knife — a relic of some kind."

Tibbs continued. "How well did you know him, sir?"

"He was a merchant with whom I dealt."

"How would you describe his personality?"

"I didn't concern myself particularly with it. He had certain things for sale in which I was interested. Those I liked enough I purchased. That was the sum and substance of it."

"I see. What is your line of work, Mr. Harvey?"

"Investments."

"Do you mean by that that you are a broker or counselor?"

"No, I am a professional trader. Do you understand me?"

"I believe so." Tibbs glanced at his watch. "Am I keeping you from your work? The market will be open another hour and a quarter, I believe."

Harvey studied him for a moment. "The market is very static today," he answered. "If anything at all breaks, my broker will call me."

Virgil probed a little. "Mr. Harvey, in your financial transactions, do you normally have access to industrial information which guides you in your decisions?"

If Harvey had shown any signs of relaxing his manner, he remedied the defect. His voice was from the Alaskan North Slope. "I do not. I simply take advantage of the amateurism of many small investors who have no clear understanding of what they are doing. Suppose you had bought Occidental Petroleum, for example, when it was in the low forties and then sold it in desperation when it dropped down to around fifteen in mid-1970; under those circumstances you would have lost a great deal of money. Thousands did. Their losses for the most part went to professional traders who had sold Oxy short. I was one of them. As long as inexperienced people think that they can play the market and profit, with limited finances and less knowledge, I will continue to make a very good living taking advantage of their weaknesses."

"That's very impressive, Mr. Harvey."

"Perhaps, but I fail to see how it will help you in your investigation."

Virgil crossed his legs and took out his notebook. "Mr. Harvey, when was the last time that you saw Mr. Wang alive?"

"Perhaps a week ago, I don't recall exactly."

"During the afternoon?"

"If you know, why ask me?"

Tibbs looked up. "I was assuming, sir, that you would stay close to your phone during market hours."

Harvey allowed the point. "Very well, it was in the afternoon. I now recall that it was six days ago."

"And you made the purchase that I just delivered to you at that time?"

"Yes."

"I presume, sir, that in view of the value of the jade and the extensive stock that Mr. Wang had, you took some time in making your selection."

"No," Harvey almost snapped. "I never require time to make up my mind. That is one of the basic principles for success in the market."

Tibbs refused to be ruffled. "Had you seen the piece that you purchased previously?"

"If I had, I would have bought it at that time. Will there be anything else?"

"Only one thing more, Mr. Harvey. If it is convenient, I would very much like to see your jade collection. I'm developing an interest in the subject."

There was a measured pause. "Do you consider this
to be part of your investigation?"

"I wouldn't have asked otherwise."

"Very well, then." Harvey rose. "Come with me."

He led the way around the corner of the L-shaped
room and then into a den which was equipped with an
electronic desk calculator. Books on financial subjects
filled one wall. On the opposite side of the small room
a glass-fronted case was mounted at eye level; in it a
dozen jade pieces were displayed. The carvings stood
in a geometric arrangement, equally spaced, facing
uniformly forward. Mr. Wang had placed his in a less
regular way and some of them had been turned a few
degrees one way or the other. The precision in this
cabinet, Tibbs noted, reflected the mind and habits of
the man who had put the pieces where they were.

Virgil studied the display for a minute or two and
then announced himself as satisfied. "If I may have a
receipt for the jade I delivered to you," he said, "I will
be on my way."

Harvey seated himself at his desk and with a pen
scribbled on a slip of paper. As soon as he had handed
it over he led the way briskly to the front door and
showed Tibbs out with the least amount of ceremony
that the situation permitted. As the door was closing
the phone began to ring.

As he drove back into Pasadena Virgil went over the interview he had just had. That done, he turned his thoughts to the girl who was living, alone now, in Mr. Wang's home. Her problem was a profoundly difficult one. Time might be the only cure — time in which she might mellow somewhat, but more importantly, time in which society might come a little closer to evaluating people for what they were and not for their origins.

He stopped across from the house and noted the still tightly closed draperies that masked the front windows. As he approached the front door he was mildly surprised to find Yumeko waiting for him. The portal was half open and the girl herself was largely hidden behind it. When he was on the step she opened it wider to admit him and accepted the receipt that he handed her. She took it in her fingers but did not even glance at it; instead, her eyes were on his face and serious concern was written across her features. "I am glad that you have returned," she said.

The conclusion was obvious, but he asked anyway. "Has something happened?"

She led him silently into the living room and once more sank into the same chair. As Tibbs seated himself where he too had been before, she turned worried eyes on him. "Two men came," she said. "Also policemen. They asked me many, many questions."

Virgil did not like that; this was his case and if any of the other boys wanted to interview one of the prin·

cipals, they should have cleared it with him first. "Did they give you a hard time?" he asked, his voice grim.

Slowly Yumeko shook her head. "Not hard. They were polite. But very persistent. They said they are coming back. I was frightened."

"Who were they?" Virgil demanded.

"Mr. Lonigan and Mr. Duffy," she answered.

CHAPTER 6

Mr. Aaron Finegold sat in his office chair with his long legs thrust out under his desk so that he was all but resting on the base of his spine. His narrow, dark face was capped by a thick mass of black, very curly hair which maintained some semblance of order only under continuous protest. His eyes were deep sunk and fairly close, giving the illusion that they were surrounded by permanent dark circles. Sometimes they appeared sleepy, on other occasions they had been known to suggest a raven with insomnia. With such strong features to support, Mr. Finegold required a nose of more than ordinary distinction and he possessed one. The total effect of his physiognomy was notable — it was an accidental part of his stock in trade.

"You wanted to see me," he said.

Virgil Tibbs had interviewed a great many people in the course of his police career, and lawyers were not new to him, in their offices or in court. He therefore looked back at Mr. Finegold with unperturbed composure. "I understand that you were the attorney for the late Mr. Wang Fu-sen."

"Yes."

Virgil laid his card on the desk. "I have been assigned to investigate his death; this necessitates some questions. May I have your cooperation?"

Finegold recognized the ploy and countered it. "I'm sure that you recognize my position and understand what I can and cannot do."

"Among the 'can's,' I trust, is helping me to find the person or persons who caused the death of your client."

That brought things to dead center. "Very well," Finegold said, "what do you want to know?"

"First of all, can you tell me if Mr. Wang had any relatives with whom I might get in touch?"

Finegold shook his head. "The only ones I know of are behind the Bamboo Curtain, and I doubt very much if they can be located or written to."

"I have the impression that he may have left a considerable estate."

"I believe that is true. At least in terms of the jade collection he had. His pieces were excellent and very valuable."

"Can you tell me, sir, if there is a will."

"Yes, and a fairly recent one."

Tibbs changed his tone somewhat. "You understand, Mr. Finegold, that inheritance is often a very powerful motive for murder."

A silent nod answered him.

"The value of Mr. Wang's estate might have encouraged someone to speed his demise."

The attorney sat up straighter in his chair. "That is true as far as it goes, but it is manifestly unfair. Putting it the way you did means that anyone and everyone who stands to benefit from Mr. Wang's unfortunate death also comes under a cloud of suspicion."

Tibbs crossed his legs. "Mr. Finegold, I didn't come here to spar with you and there is no jury to be impressed either way. I'm solely interested in finding out who killed your client and why."

"All right, let's go on from that premise. What next?"

"On another topic for a moment: do you have any knowledge, or suspicion, that Mr. Wang might have been in any way involved in the narcotics trade?"

That brought his host up straight in his chair once more. "I'll give you a direct and unequivocated answer to that: absolutely not." He paused a moment before he continued. "I assume that you are not subject to racial prejudices against minorities."

Virgil looked at him, but said nothing.

"It's not precisely accurate to describe the Chinese as a minority, but they are in this country," Finegold went on. "However there are plenty of people ready to attribute to them certain classic vices that they are supposed to favor."

"It's my turn to avoid equivocation," Tibbs answered. "I asked you that question because I had a specific reason for doing so. That is confidential information and I will ask you to regard it as such."

Finegold surveyed him carefully. "Let me ask you something off the record if I may: if Mr. Wang were alive and well today, is there any possibility that he might be in jeopardy in connection with illegal drugs?"

"Truthfully, I don't know. At the moment it is enough of a possibility that I'm checking it out. Mr. Wang does not stand accused posthumously as of now, or if he does, I am unaware of it."

"Then let me say this: Francis Wang was as fine and honorable a gentleman as I have ever known in my life. I cannot even conceive of his having an enemy, although it is patent that he had one, at least. He was my trusted supplier of fine Chinese lapidary work, my client, and my valued friend."

"Francis?"

"Many Chinese, Mr. Tibbs, realizing that their names are sometimes difficult for Westerners, take an anglicized first name to make things simpler. Particularly if they are in any form of trade."

"If your relationship was as you suggest, and I don't question that, may I ask why you seemed reluctant at first to discuss the matter with me? You fully understood the purpose of my visit."

Finegold leaned back in his chair. "You have me cornered on that one and I will have to be candid with you. I am interested in protecting Mr. Wang's reputation, even after his demise, and I had that in mind. In addition, there is another consideration. You're going to find this out anyway so I might as well inform you now. Francis asked me to represent Miss Yumeko Nagashima only a week or so ago. Do you know this young lady?"

Tibbs nodded. "Yes, I've had that pleasure. You'd better tell me what kind of difficulty she's in."

"None that I'm aware of."

"You just told me that Mr. Wang asked you to represent her. Normally he would hardly do that for a houseguest without some reason."

"Mr. Tibbs, I hope that I'm never placed in the position of having to defend a guilty client in court against you. Miss Nagashima is something of an enigma; I don't know a great deal about her background, only that Francis Wang befriended her and very obviously was glad that he had done so. I seriously question that there was any sexual relationship between them and I also strongly doubt that there was any blood relationship."

Virgil nodded. "I agree on both counts, at least as of now. That's based on personal judgment and nothing else."

"Good. That's as far as I feel that I can take it at this time, but since I have been retained, even though very informally, to look after Miss Nagashima, I had her interests in mind when we were talking earlier."

Tibbs locked his fingers and then pressed them until they seemed to grow white. "Mr. Finegold, I understand your reluctance to continue and I believe I know the reason for it. I want to ask you one more question nonetheless."

"I'll answer it if I feel that I can."

"Very well. I believe you anticipate what it is now. You have already informed me that Mr. Wang made a recent will. And that he asked you, also very recently, to protect Miss Nagashima's interests. And you have stated that to the best of your knowledge she was not in any difficulty at that time." He looked up. "The inference is, of course, perfectly obvious. Was, or is, Miss Nagashima mentioned in that will?"

For several seconds the subdued hum of an electric clock on the desk was the only real sound in the room. When Finegold spoke, his voice was controlled. "I will answer that question with the understanding that the information is for your private use only as a police officer until such time as it is made public."

"Agreed, with the proviso that it may be necessary to discuss it within the police department to a limited degree."

"Accepted. Very well, then: Mr. Wang made a number of provisions of a personal and also a charitable nature. He left certain assets to his family association. After that what was left, and I would say that it is considerable, goes in its entirety to Miss Nagashima. She does not know this, or didn't at the time. In particular the considerable treasure that Mr. Wang's jade collection represents will all be hers."

"Thank you, Mr. Finegold; no wonder you were

retained to protect her interests. I am frankly amazed to discover that she is an heiress."

The attorney got to his feet. "No more so than I was, Mr. Tibbs, when I was asked to draw up that document. But Francis was, in his quiet way, totally determined, and there was no point in arguing with him. Somehow, in some way, that girl had become someone very important in his life."

The Bureau of Narcotics and Dangerous Drugs advised over the phone that both Mr. Lonigan and Mr. Duffy were out and could not be conveniently reached. Expecting that that would be the case, Virgil left his number, 577–4598, and then returned to his car. He drove, slowly and thoughtfully, to the municipal library and went inside.

The reference librarian knew him well, as she had cause to. "What will it be this time, Mr. Tibbs?" she asked. "You won't surprise me with anything."

Virgil smiled. "What have you on jade?" he asked.

"Oh, quite a bit. Are you interested in the stone itself, in jewelry, in American jade, or Chinese carvings?"

"Chinese carvings — definitely."

"Oh yes, I remember reading about that in the paper. Of course it would be your case." She rose. "I don't remember the author's name, but there is a very good book on the subject that was recently reprinted.

Someone else was in here asking about it very recently."

She led the way to the catalog and quickly located the cards that she wanted. "There are a number of works available, some of them very technical. As an introduction, I think I'd recommend *The Stone of Heaven* by Gump. After that you'll want — yes, here it is — *Chinese Jade Throughout the Ages* by Nott. Now I just hope that they're in. Nott is a standard work and the one I was telling you about."

Ten minutes later Tibbs left the library bearing two volumes — a fairly slender one and a second which was much more substantial. When he got back to his office Bob Nakamura was out, but as he put the books down he saw the note Bob had left for him in the center of his desk. *Call Chief McGowan as soon as you get in.*

It took a few seconds for the call to be completed. When it was, McGowan's quiet, unruffled voice came over the line. "Come on up, Virgil. A couple of gentlemen are here who have been waiting to talk with you."

Tibbs knew immediately who the gentlemen in question were. It seemed to him, for just a moment, that they could not leave either himself or the case he was working on alone, and he was annoyed. Then he got hold of himself and remembered that if they had not come to see him, it would have been the other way around. All they had done was to save him some trouble.

As he walked into the chief's office, both Lonigan and Duffy got to their feet and shook hands. "I'm glad to see you," Virgil said truthfully. "I've been trying to get in touch with you."

"We've heard," Duffy responded. "We were expecting that you'd call. Our paths seem to have crossed quite abruptly."

"Since you gentlemen obviously want to compare notes, why don't you use the conference room?" McGowan said. "It's available. Let me know if you arrive at any decisions."

As he walked out toward the conference room Tibbs saw once more the face of Yumeko when she had told him about her visit from the federal narcotics agents. Her dismay had been too real to have been put on; she had been genuinely shaken up. Now he intended to find out why.

When the door had been closed, Lonigan opened the conversation.

"When we first talked to you, Mr. Tibbs, we didn't foresee that Wang Fu-sen was going to die violently that same day and that you would handle the case."

"It's one helluva coincidence," Virgil said, and looked a question mark at him.

"Yes and no. Coincidence that the man died just when he did, not so remarkable that you were assigned to it. You're the top homicide man here."

Something in his tone suggested that the sentence was not complete in itself. "Are you telling me," Tibbs asked, "that Chief McGowan was aware of your interest in that man?"

"Before we asked for you," Duffy said, "We leveled with him. Naturally — he's the boss."

"All the way?"

"A good part of it."

"Then why wasn't I told?" Tibbs asked.

"You are being told — now. You've been a little busy, and so have we."

Virgil sat down and stretched his legs under the table. "I think it would be a good idea if we had a friendly understanding. You've got a damned important job to do — and so have I. The difference is that I can finalize and you can't. So I should be out of the picture, hopefully, before too long. In the meantime, for God's sake, let's not get in each other's way!"

"Amen to that," Lonigan said, and sat down too. "I know what's on your mind — we were out talking to that girl — Nagashima."

"Let me have it," Tibbs said. "What have you got on her?"

Duffy dropped into one of the vacant chairs. "Your name's Virgil, isn't it? All right, Virgil, the straight answer is that we don't know."

"On Wang himself?"

"We don't know that either."

"Well, for your information, gentlemen, you scared

the pee out of her and then left her with the happy thought that you were coming back."

Lonigan became tougher. "We are, unless we are absolutely satisfied about something and convinced that she's in the clear. That isn't the case right now."

"What are the odds that she's implicated?"

"No bet."

Virgil's voice acquired a snap that more than matched Lonigan's. "A few hours ago you were inviting me to work with you, now you're holding out on me while I'm engaged in a murder investigation. If it works out that that girl killed her benefactor, and she's convicted of it in court, then she could be sentenced to the gas chamber. That's about as serious as you can get. You had a right to go and see her, but in doing so you messed me up but good. Now I suggest that we lay a few cards on the table so that we stop working at cross purposes."

Duffy calmed things down. "You're right, Virgil, I can't dispute that. I suggest that we *do* work together; we'll put you in the picture if you, in turn, will give us what help you can with what we're up against."

"All right. Let's have it."

Lonigan began. "Generally there are three sources for the illegal narcotics and drugs that are on the market: the Middle East via France, Mexico, and the Far East. Most of the heroin that feeds into the East Coast originates in Turkey as opium; it's converted to morphine in Lebanon and in turn into heroin in southeastern France, usually in or around Marseilles. Heroin also comes up from Mexico, but it's usually of much poorer quality; it's consumed for the most part in California and some in Hawaii. The price has gone well above four hundred and fifty dollars an ounce, and that's for a diluted product."

"I know most of this," Virgil said.

"I assumed that you did, but I've got a reason for going over it now. There are certain prime ports in Southeast Asia that are shipping out illegal drugs to this country. They include Bangkok, Penang, and Singapore. Much of it, in the form of solid blocks of morphine trademarked 999, is shipped to Hong Kong. There the conversion to heroin is done. At one step in the process, if the stuff is heated a little too much, the whole place can blow up. That happens, every now and then."

"That should help a little with the control problem."

"I'd like to think that it does. But now let me put some pieces together for you: the chief sources for jade carvings are also Hong Kong, Singapore, and to a lesser degree Bangkok. For a while jade wasn't allowed to come into the United States, but our late friend Mr. Wang managed to keep supplied. Or so we are reliably informed. And there is some supporting evidence that the narcotics traders have been in frequent contact with him; we have that pretty well established as a matter of fact. Then, just at a crucial period, the young lady now living in his home arrived from the Orient and took up residence with him for no visible reason. And no sooner was she here than the supply began to increase."

Tibbs interrupted with a question. "Is this circumstantial so far, or do you have any direct evidence?"

"Nothing direct — as yet. Now two more things that may help to focus the picture a little. Literally every day hundreds of tons of imports of all kinds arrive in this country; it's a physical impossibility to search every shipment thoroughly for contraband, so we rely very heavily on informants overseas. We stop a lot of stuff that way. Not all, of course. Some of the information we have been getting pointed to Wang. That's definite."

Duffy picked up. "The big kicker we've been saving for last. You'd better brace yourself for this one."

"Go ahead."

"Let me ask you: what's worse than horse — heroin?"

"Nothing that I know of," Tibbs answered. "In some cases LSD because of the unpredictable after-effects. The fact that the user can take off on another trip anytime, without warning, weeks or months after the most recent use of the drug."

"True, but LSD isn't truly addictive. I'm talking now about drugs of pure addiction."

"On that basis, heroin heads the list."

Duffy shook his head. "It used to, out not anymore. Have you ever heard of keto-bedmidone? Or Claradon, that's another name for it."

Virgil shook his head.

Lonigan folded his hands on top of the table. "It's a synthetic, made and used in Europe for certain very limited medical purposes. It's a powerful analgesic which can be administered for the relief of extreme pain, say to a person who has been badly mangled in an accident and isn't expected to live."

"How about Demerol?"

"There are lots of things that can do the job; keto-bedmidone is one of them. But it has two other properties that make it extremely dangerous. First, it produces significant euphoria, in addicts' language a tremendous high. And it is extremely addictive. Considerably more than heroin."

"In other words, it outdoes heroin all the way?"

"In broad terms, you could put it that way."

"It must be hellish stuff," Tibbs said.

"It is. It's completely banned in this country, but recently it has turned up here. I doubt if many junkies, knowing what it is, would risk it themselves, and you know what they do to their bodies."

"I've seen some things."

Lonigan paused, as though he was choosing his next words with great care. "Virgil, we have it that the Chicoms have been making this stuff and that they have definite plans for introducing it into this country in quantity. They know what it can do."

Tibbs had a question. "Frank, gone as the junkies are most of the time, they have some brains when they're normal. As long as they can get heroin, do you think that they would lay themselves open to anything like this?"

Lonigan nodded. "That's our hope. They got wise to speed and eased up on it. If any more of this stuff gets on the market, then we'll put out the word and do it fast. Of course there's a small percentage of drug users who'll try anything just to prove how brave they are. They play Russian roulette with their lives all the time. Have you heard of fruit salad?"

Virgil was grim. "We brought two of them into Huntington Memorial last month. One terminal, one made it by the grace of God and a stomach pump. About keto-bedmidone; have you any idea when it's supposed to be coming in?"

"No, we don't have that. Only some pretty solid information from Hong Kong that it would be on its way, and that the late Mr. Wang would be the recipient. Or the girl; she may have been planted there for that purpose. So you see now why we're so interested in that young lady."

When Tibbs got back to his office Bob Nakamura was there. He was catching up on paper work, mountains of which cleared through the department every month. It seemed that police administration had to be buttressed by a phalanx of paper or it would not operate.

"After all these years I ought to be getting used to you, Virg," he said, looking up from his typewriter, "but you never cease to amaze me. I've been in touch with the morgue. How in the hell did you know that that stone implement sticking out of the late Mr. Wang Fu-sen's chest probably wasn't the cause of his death? You were right, but I have it from Floyd Sanderson that all you did was kneel down and look at the body passively for two or three minutes."

Tibbs shrugged. "If you'd been there, you would have seen it too."

"I'm not so sure; armed robbery is more my line. Anyhow, what was the gimmick?"

"First, please tell me how the man died."

"That's the funny part, Virg; they aren't sure yet. Apparently somebody may have stabbed him with it after he was dead."

"That was my conclusion." Tibbs said dryly.

"All right, wonder boy, open up. What gave it to you?"

"The position of the body principally, that was the major factor. Once that suggested the idea, several other things contributed."

"Such as?"

"Have you seen the pictures?"

"Not yet."

"Go look at them. If you have any questions after that, we'll talk about it."

"You don't want to discuss it now."

"That's right; I've got another idea I want to think about. Forgive me, will you?"

"Of course. When you get an idea, I usually keep out of the way."

Tibbs looked at his own desk and shook his head in despair. "It isn't anything tremendous right now — at least not on the surface. It may never be. But I think, in the interests of duty, of course, that I'm going to take a lady to dinner."

"Miss Nagashima?"

"Yes, if that's who she really is. The Feds had a go at her this morning, but when I talked to them, they were notably mum about what went on. I have a few innocuous questions I'd like to ask her myself. In a nice way, of course."

Nakamura looked at him. "Heaven help her," he said.

CHAPTER 7

When Virgil Tibbs pulled up at six-thirty almost to the minute in front of the house of the late Wang Fu-sen, he was driving his own car. He had changed into a pair of two-tone slacks and a sport coat; to complete his ensemble he had chosen a light-blue shirt and one of the new wide ties considerably bolder in design than those he wore during business hours. He walked up the driveway quite unconcerned about what the neighbors might think, and rang the bell.

It was a few seconds before Yumeko opened the door. When she did, Tibbs experienced a pleasant surprise; she had on a simple black dress which displayed her figure to considerable advantage. On it she wore an exquisite jade clip in the form of a long-tailed bird of almost living realism. The otherwise unadorned dress set off her very rich dark eyes, her black hair, and the deep hue of her skin. As Virgil surveyed her, he appreciated for the first time that she was, in her way, exotically beautiful.

"Good evening," he said.

Yumeko welcomed him inside. "I thank you for asking me," she said formally. It was very proper, perfectly polite, and remotely cynical. The hint was so slight that Tibbs was not sure whether he had read it correctly or not; her familiarity with English was remarkably good for a Japanese, but it was as yet far from perfect. He told himself not to try to read subtle nuances in her speech, remembering that she was expressing herself in what was to her a complex and very difficult foreign language.

"I'm glad you could come," he responded. He wanted to banish the stiffness, but it was too early. She had been raised under a different culture in a different environment; more than that, she was not yet over the shock of violent death and cold murder. At that moment he did not believe that she had, with her own hands, struck down her benefactor, but his experience told him not to allow his personal inclinations to prejudice the objectivity of his work. He was more than stretching a point by taking a definite suspect out to dinner; he had justified it to himself by assuming that under social circumstances it might be easier to obtain some added information from her, but he knew that he had been rationalizing.

"Is it that you wish to go now?" she asked.

He gave her a half smile and said, "Why not." As he

walked beside her to his car he was aware that she was not very tall. After he opened the door he noted the way in which she seated herself; she had a natural ease of movement despite the fact that she was far from being relaxed.

He got in behind the wheel and then turned to her. "Would you enjoy a Japanese dinner?" he asked.

When she looked back at him he noticed how large her eyes were despite their Oriental configuration. "You can eat?" she asked.

He noted the change in grammar and correctly guessed that she had translated literally from the Japanese. "Yes, of course," he said. "I like it."

He started the engine and began to drive toward the center of the city. He sensed that his companion was not interested in small talk, so he remained silent. In the back of his mind was the nagging thought that by inviting Yumeko Nagashima for dinner and the evening he was overstepping the bounds of police discretion. But he could not withdraw now; the girl was in the car beside him and his duty was clear.

The restaurant he had selected was located in the semibasement of a substantial building not far from police headquarters. After the few concrete steps which led down to the entrance the atmosphere changed abruptly; with the Japanese genius for creating tranquil decorations in even the smallest space, the little foyer had been made attractive and inviting. Inside, the restaurant itself calmly ignored the prosaic streets outside and contented itself with being a small corner of the Orient where food was served.

The hostess, appropriately clad in a pink flowered kimono, received them, checked her reservation sheet, and then guided them to a table in the dining room. "I'm sorry," she said, "I should have asked you. Would you prefer to have your dinner in the tatami room?"

Virgil looked at his companion and waited for her to answer. "I believe," Yumeko said, in carefully phrased English, "that Mr. Tibbs might be more happy here."

The hostess looked at her once again and then, motioning for them to sit down, added a welcome in Japanese. The effect on Yumeko was visible: she replied at once, obviously grateful for the opportunity to speak her own language even if only briefly. To Tibbs the conversation was incomprehensible, but he noted the difference in Yumeko — in her sudden ease of speech and relaxation of manner. It was as though she had become a different person.

When the hostess had left, some of the warmth remained. "She is very nice person," Yumeko said. "She gave us a fine welcome. She forgives me my birth, I think because her husband is *hakojin*. I am sorry — that means that he is a Caucasian."

Virgil wanted to say something to her then about her ancestry, but he remained silent. There would be time enough for that later. Instead he picked up the menu and consumed a quarter of a minute in making his decision. "What would you like to have?" he asked.

Before she could reply a cocktail waitress appeared at their table and inquired about drinks. Yumeko shook her head. "Please, no," she said. After Tibbs had declined for himself, she explained. "Once I became sorry for myself and had much to drink. I became very sick and my stomach reversed itself. Now I do not wish it anymore."

"That's as good a reason as any," Virgil said. "Why do it if you don't like it."

Yumeko shot him a quick glance at that and continued to study his features for several more seconds. She said nothing, however, and picked up the menu. It hid her face while she scanned it and decided what she would like to have.

"You do not mind if I eat real Japanese food?" she inquired.

"That's why I brought you here."

When the waitress came she ordered in Japanese. There was some small discussion and then it was Tibbs' turn. "Sukiyaki," he said simply.

"Gohan?"

He looked blankly at her.

"I beg your pardon — would you like rice?"

"Please."

The waitress produced an electric stove and plugged it in, ready for the ritual of cooking the sukiyaki at the table. Then she brought clear thin soup in dark lacquer bowls and set down tiny dishes of Japanese pickles. She placed a pair of wrapped chopsticks beside Yumeko and provided Tibbs with both a set of sticks and conventional silverware.

Yumeko picked up her soup bowl, ready to drink from the rim. "I thank you for giving me this meal," she said. "I have not had Japanese food very recently."

"I'm glad you could come," Virgil responded. He studied his companion and tried to understand her. To him she was Japanese: she spoke the language and had grown up under that culture. Yet he was aware that she was half Negro and the tone of her skin was much like his own. He was unable to decide in his mind whether her difficulty lay in her mixed heritage per se, or in the fairly obvious fact that her parents had not been man and wife. As he sipped his soup he reflected on the point, then deliberately put it aside.

The waitress arrived with a platter of artfully arranged ingredients for the sukiyaki and a plain iron cooking utensil in which to prepare it. "What are you having?" Tibbs asked.

In reply Yumeko gestured toward the ample platter of meat and vegetables.

"I don't understand Japanese, you know that," he continued, "but I didn't hear you order it."

"I at first order something else," she explained. "Then when you order sukiyaki, I changed so as to be the same as you."

"Why?"

"It is more polite. Also it is easier for the waitress."

He looked at her carefully once more and wondered if she were capable of committing murder. There were strange combinations in human beings, he knew that well, but Yumeko was an enigma.

He contented himself with watching while the waitress cooked their main course and then, with her own chopsticks, deftly served them initial portions in small bowls. Another girl arrived with a container of boiled rice and then came once more with tea. The service was smooth and efficient, just a trifle better than usual, perhaps, because one of the guests was at least partly Japanese.

The food was very good, enough so that it remained largely a silent meal while they ate. Virgil had little to say and Yumeko clearly had no intention of initiating any conversation. One thing he had been considering was the thought that she was entirely content to accept him as her escort. That in itself was of some significance; it indicated to him that she did not attach the sins of her father onto all others who shared his origins. Perhaps she felt herself to be at least in part a Negro girl after all and if so, that was all to the good.

A little less than an hour later, as they were leaving the restaurant, he wondered quite suddenly what his next move ought to be. He had kept the matter out of his mind, but now it confronted him and he had to make a decision. He was rapidly weighing whether he ought to suggest a movie or else take her home when the girl herself resolved the matter for him. "Where do you live?" she asked.

"Not far from here. I have an apartment."

"You have roommate?"

"No, I live alone. There are several other police officers in the same building."

For just a moment Yumeko stood stock still as though preparing herself for something. Then she said, "We go to your rooms now?"

That surprised him; for a moment he was off balance. "Would you like to do that?" he asked.

"Let us go," she answered him, and turned in the direction of his parked car.

Tibbs thought hard during the short drive, aware that to a small degree he had been trapped. Taking the girl to dinner had perhaps been an indiscretion to begin with; he could not understand why he had issued the invitation in the first place. Obviously he had not been thinking clearly, or had not thought at all. Now he was committed to taking her to his apartment. The morals of the situation did not bother him at all; Cotton Mather had been out of the picture for some time. It was his own position as the investigating officer that had him worried; if it was her idea to offer herself to him in return for full or partial immunity of one kind or another, he would have no choice but to take her home in an atmosphere that would be anything but pleasant. And to treat her with glacial reserve from that moment forward.

He decided to play it by ear. He pulled his car up in front of the attractively landscaped two-story apartment building, got out, and then held the car door open for her. He watched carefully as she let him help her to her feet, trying to read a visible clue in her behavior. For those few seconds, however, she remained completely Japanese and gave him no hint whatsoever. She walked behind him to the lobby of the building, then followed as he led her to the second-floor apartment that he called home. He inserted a key, reached inside to turn on the lights, then stepped aside to allow her to enter.

She walked in a few steps, stopped, and then looked about her. The living room was in good condition; the cleaning lady had been in that day and had left things able to pass feminine inspection. The furniture, while not elaborate, was tasteful and of good quality. The room had been designed for comfort, not for show, and it appeared to better advantage as a result.

"It is very nice," Yumeko said. Then she turned and for the first time saw the opposite wall. It was dominated by a magnificent painting, executed with such a remarkable use of color that it seemed to be almost radiant with its own light. It showed a vital, attractive nude young woman in an outdoor setting. Her finely formed head and features were set off by blond hair which had been captured with startling fidelity by the artist despite the fact that his rendition was not entirely literal. She looked out from the canvas with a clear and steady poise that was magnetic. The sunlight seemed to reflect from her bare shoulders while her firm, sculptured breasts underlined her femininity. The whole portrait appeared almost to possess a life of its own, once seen it commanded attention and retained it with a compelling power.

Yumeko studied it. "It is very beautiful," she said carefully. "The painter, I think, he is very exceptionally good."

Tibbs stood quietly and waited. "That he certainly is. William Holt-Rymers."

"I do not know this name." Yumeko still kept her attention on the picture. "But it is no difference. He is famous anyway — he must be."

"He is very well known."

"The girl," she said presently, "she is real I think."

"Yes, she is."

"You know her?"

Virgil nodded. "Yes, her name is Linda. Linda Nunn."

Yumeko looked at him for the first time. "You have seen her this way?"

"Yes, I have."

Quietly and with total composure Yumeko walked to the davenport and sat down. "She is your girl friend, I think also."

Tibbs looked at her calmly. "No, Yumeko, she isn't.

I know her, but that's as far as it goes — for many reasons." He changed the subject. "You told me that you don't drink, but can I offer you any kind of refreshment? Something you might like?"

She clasped her hands in her lap. "If you can give me something that will not make me sick, I think I would like to have it. It would help me."

He did not fully understand that, but he nodded anyway and stepped behind his small bar in the corner of the room. "I think that I know something. If you don't care for it, just set it aside."

He reached for a bottle and uncorked it. That done he put some ice in a glass and poured out a ruby-red beverage. He carried it over to her and waited while she tasted it.

"It is very good, I like this."

"Good," he responded. He fixed a second similar drink for himself and then sat down, beside her but not intimately close. "Let me tell you about the picture. It was given to me by the artist after I completed a murder investigation in which both he and Miss Nunn were involved."*

"He made it especially for you?"

"Yes, he did. And Linda posed for the same reason."

Yumeko tried her drink once more. "What is this?" she asked.

"Cherry Heering."

* *The Cool Cottontail.* Ed.

"It is good," she said once more. Then she looked again at the portrait. "After you are knowing her, I am ashamed; I will be a disappointment for you."

Virgil looked at her with some concern. "I don't understand."

Yumeko lifted her shoulders slightly and then let them fall. "I do not possess such a body as that. I am woman, yes, but half Japanese. Therefore I am smaller across the chest. I am sorry, but I cannot help it."

Very carefully, and taking his time, Tibbs tasted a little of his own drink. Then when he spoke his voice was under careful control. "Yumeko, did you come here with the idea of going to bed with me?"

Her eyes were open and challenging. "Is it not for this that you asked me to come with you?"

"And you accepted on that basis?" he asked.

She resigned herself. "Of course. My mother instructed me about this country. We have our customs in Japan, you have yours also. I understand this." She picked up her glass.

"All right." Virgil turned until he was facing her squarely. "Now I will explain something to you. I asked you out, when I knew that I shouldn't, because I felt sorry for what had happened to you and I wanted to give you a little pleasure. And because I thought that you would be good company. Do you understand that?"

"Yes, I do."

He drummed his fingers against the back of the

sofa. "Now I go to bed with girls when I have the opportunity and things are right — I think that almost every normal man does. But for me just to buy you a dinner and then expect you to come through — I mean to go to bed with me — just because of that would be . . ." He paused and tried to find a word. ". . . Ungentlemanly."

Yumeko continued to look at him. "You did not expect?" she asked.

"Of course not. I asked you out for your company and that's all."

"But you know what I am!"

That settled it; he had felt sure that he knew what was eating her, but he had tried to dismiss it. Now it was there in front of him and he would have to deal with it.

"Yumeko," he said, "I want you to come over here and sit beside me."

Calmly, and without emotion, she obeyed.

When she had settled herself against him, and he could feel both the warmth and the tightness of her body, he laid his arm across her shoulders and waited a few seconds until he could feel the first indication of relaxation — of her acceptance of the situation.

"Now I'm going to lecture to you and I want you to listen," he said. "Don't interrupt me until I'm through — do you understand?"

She nodded her head, which seemed suddenly small beside his shoulder.

"My ancestors, whoever they were, came to this country from Africa some time ago. Not as you came, they were slaves; they were bought and sold like cattle, worked like hell in most cases, and were often raped. Then the country came a little farther up the road and that was done away with. After that all we had to do was to try and prove that we were human beings who were capable of doing normal things and that our color didn't run off onto everything that we touched. You ought to know all this, because half of your background is the same as mine."

He took a little more of his drink. "It isn't all over yet, of course, but if we can keep the militants from making us hated everywhere we show our faces, it's getting better every day. The job I have, the fact that it was given to me, means something and you ought to know that."

He took a deep breath. "For centuries humanity has been living in little pockets all over the world; people kept to themselves because travel was difficult, or all but impossible. Nobody from here went to Japan, for example, for quite a long while."

"It was not allowed," Yumeko said.

"I know, that's part of it. Then came the airplane and later the jet engine. That changed everything; now you, or anyone else, can go to almost any part of the world in a matter of hours. People are meeting each other, mixing as they never did before."

He felt her go tight again. "I know this — I understand. But that does not help me. I am what I became and I cannot be anything else. And everyone knows."

He did not mean to, but he tightened his arm across her shoulder until she was almost in pain. "Yumeko, dammit, don't be so stubborn! Try to understand. A century ago — that's one hundred years — anyone like you would have been very strange, *but it isn't true anymore*. A century ago I couldn't have been what I am now; people would have thought me some kind of an animal that could be trained to do certain tricks, like shining shoes."

"But at least you were one kind of animal!"

Tibbs controlled himself and regained his self possession. "And so are you," he answered, "whether you know it or not. You're all human, all girl. I know you're a hybrid; so is all the best corn — they raise it that way." He turned her around until she had to look at him. "How many people alive today, do you think, have absolutely pure blood of one kind or another? Not that many. And they're not the lucky ones, because when you start mixing strains you get a better product most of the time. In horses, in plants, and in human beings too."

He took hold of both her shoulders and his fingers almost dug into her flesh. "You're lucky as all hell and you don't know it. The chances of any one person being born are billions to one against. The odds are dreadful even with the same set of parents. You beat all those odds and against a fearful handicap. Just remember that it took a miracle to make you alive, but here you are. Now enjoy it!"

He let her go and got to his feet. "I think I'd better take you back now," he concluded. "Tomorrow is going to be a tough day and I have a murderer to catch."

He took her to her door. As he stood one step down to bid her good-night their heads were on a level. As he looked at her then he thought that she was damned attractive and she ought to know it. But he left it at that. She was still right in the middle of his investigation and his promise to himself that he was going to use part of the evening to get some further information out of her lay shattered.

"Keep your door locked," he advised her, "and don't let anybody in unless you know who they are. Even then be careful."

On that stern note he turned his back and left. There had been murder done in that house and until he knew why and how, the shadow would hang dark and heavy over it and the girl who had just gone inside. Disturbed in his mind for many reasons, and with his self-confidence definitely shaken, he went back to his car.

CHAPTER 8

When he checked in for work the following morning, Virgil Tibbs did not choose to remain in his office for very long. He had many things to do, in addition to which he did not welcome the idea that someone might drop in to ask him how he had enjoyed his date with one of his ranking suspects on the previous evening. News got around the Pasadena Police Department much as it did everywhere else; if anyone at all had seen him while he had had Yumeko in tow, everyone would know about it as a matter of course.

Fortunately no one came in to raise the issue; he was therefore able to dispose of a small pile of urgent paper work. Then he picked up his phone and rang the morgue.

He was advised that the report on the late Mr. Wang was ready; furthermore the pathologist who had performed the autopsy was on hand in case there were any questions.

Virgil did not particularly care for the morgue, but his duty took him to it often enough that the place was no novelty. When he got there he sat down in a small room with a tall, unconcerned young doctor who had probed the internal organs of the deceased. On the small, plain table which stood in the center of the room there was a carefully written document which told of the cause of death of the Chinese jade merchant and, almost conspicuously out of place, the antique stone implement which had been thrust into his chest.

"I'd like to know something," the doctor said as he lit a cigarette. "How did you arrive at the opinion that the deceased had sustained injuries before he was stabbed?"

"By some external evidence. What did you find?"

"He had been roughed up prior to his demise. He was throttled for one thing, but not enough to leave evident marks that were readily visible. He was also struck on the jaw and on the left temple."

"Did this physical abuse cause his death?"

"I won't attempt to answer that until we complete some more tests — the present report is preliminary."

"Is it possible that the blows could have produced unconsciousness?"

"Oh, yes."

"Sustained?"

"I'd say so. Remember that the deceased was an old man and in general terms probably in frail health.

Nothing radically wrong with him that we've discovered so far, but he obviously didn't take much exercise and didn't have a lot of reserves to draw on."

"One more thing: how much force did it take to drive the stone knife into the body?"

"A moderate amount; I can't define it exactly unless you want me to take the weapon and make some cadaver tests. I could do that."

Virgil shook his head. "I don't think we'll need that if what I have in mind works out. One more question: was he initially attacked from in front or behind?"

"Behind. It's in the report."

"Thanks much." Tibbs got to his feet. "I thought that he was. I appreciate your time."

"Not at all. If you want the weapon, you know the routine for signing it out."

In the lobby Virgil consulted the business card which Johnny Wu had given to him and then picked up the counter telephone. He found his man in and cooperative.

"If you want to talk some more, fine," Wu told him. "How about meeting me at the Dynasty Club at eleven? It'll be open then and not too crowded."

"Good," Tibbs told him. "I want to get an opinion from you on something I'll have with me."

Since he had plenty of time, he drove down the Pasadena Freeway almost leisurely, found a spot open in the New Chinatown area, and flipped down the visor to identify the police vehicle. Then, still forty minutes ahead of his appointment, he entered the elaborately decorated commercial area which had been designed for tourist appeal and began to study the shop windows.

Few of the stores had any jade on display and those that did for the most part showed what even to his unpracticed eye was inferior merchandise. Some of the offerings were of a uniform, rather sickly shade of green which suggested that they had been dyed. He saw nothing at first that in any way compared with the lapidary treasures in Mr. Wang's home. The more he saw, the more he came to appreciate the quality of Mr. Wang's offerings. At the same time, even the relatively poor pieces he was seeing had their effect on him; when he spotted one or two that were better, the subtle allure of jade began to stir him. In Bamboo Lane he found a shop, heavily protected with burglar alarm systems, which displayed several carvings of obviously superior worth. They appeared in some cases to be of different materials, but there was no identification and no prices were shown. Since the store was closed there was little that he could learn there, but he wished that he might have gone inside.

He had never visited the Dynasty Club, but he had heard of it — a thoroughly plush private facility operated largely for the benefit of the Asian-American community's business and political leaders. It was the sort of place the average tourist would never suspect existed, which was probably what the management and clientele desired. A phone book gave him the location; as he rode up in the elevator he wondered about the package in his left hand. It appeared very ordinary, but the effect of unwrapping it in the Dynasty Club might prove to be something quite different.

When he touched the bell before the closed door, he had to wait only a few seconds before he was greeted by a hostess who, despite the early hour, was attractively gowned and turned out.

"Good morning, sir," she said, "can I help you?"

Virgil caught her manner at once; he was not a member, but her courtesy toward him was quite genuine — she was no more concerned that he was a Negro than he was especially aware that she was an Oriental.

"I have an appointment with Mr. Wu," Tibbs said. "He asked me to meet him here."

"Of course, please come in." She opened the door wider. "Your name, sir?"

"Virgil Tibbs."

"Thank you, Mr. Tibbs. I'll see if Mr. Wu is here."

That told him immediately that the Dynasty Club was well run. He waited a minute or two while he looked about at the decor; it was very good, as he had expected that it would be. When the hostess came back she motioned to him to follow and then led him through the interior to a small dining cove where Johnny Wu was on his feet waiting for him.

"Glad to see you again. Please sit down. I know it's early, but the sun has been over the yardarm for some time. Name it."

"Is a Coke OK?"

"Of course." He addressed the hostess. "Two Cokes and some breakfast rolls. Coffee for me too. Virgil?"

Tibbs shook his head. "Just the Coke."

Johnny waved a hand in polite dismissal. "What's the latest word?" he asked.

Carefully, and without dramatics, Virgil unwrapped his package. When at last the stone knife lay revealed, he put it carefully on the center of the table midway between them and then sat back, saying nothing.

Wu looked at it for several seconds. "May I pick it up?" he asked.

"Certainly."

The lighting in the booth was subdued, but it was adequate. For at least a full minute Johnny Wu turned the ancient implement over in his hands, studying it from every angle, but always holding it with what was clearly deep respect. When he had finished he put it down with visible care and then waited while the refreshments were served. The waitress was surprisingly tall for an Oriental and also strikingly attractive. Her costume was definitely designed to display beautifully formed legs, but managed to be subdued at the same time.

"Where do you get them?" Tibbs asked.

"The girls?"

"Yes."

Johnny smiled. "It's amazing, Virgil, what you can find if you only know where to look. Most of the girls here are Japanese, and they're handpicked. You never see them on the street, but they can be found."

"Obviously somebody knows where to look."

"The club is managed by people who know their business. We have a matched set here that's especially nice — they're all taller than you might expect and quite charming."

"What is the degree of their availability?" Tibbs asked.

Johnny shook his head. "No dice, not as far as the club is concerned, at any rate. They're all nice young ladies — and I'm not saying that just because you're the law."

Virgil smiled, and drank a good half of his Coke. "Now, to business. I'd appreciate an opinion from you concerning that object." He nodded toward the stone knife.

Johnny looked at him shrewdly. "Certainly you know quite a bit about it already or you wouldn't have brought it to me."

"I think so," Tibbs admitted. "But I like to be sure about things. Especially in areas that are new to me."

"All right, I'll take it from the top. It's a ritual jade implement called a *Ya-Chang*. It's very ancient, before the Han Dynasty I'd say offhand — well before.

There's some crystallization along one of the edges which establishes this. My preliminary opinion is that it is genuine, extremely rare, and very valuable. Now it's your turn."

"It may disturb you to know this," Virgil said. "But that weapon was extracted from the chest of Mr. Wang. That is, most of it was." He stopped and waited, watching the reaction.

Johnny Wu folded his hands and looked steadily at the *Ya-Chang*. "Wang Fu-sen was my good friend. In addition to that he was a man of exceptional character and great wisdom. If I could find the man who killed him, I would gladly take that jade knife and treat him in the same manner — and to hell with the consequences."

Virgil finished his Coke. "I have a better idea," he said. "Help me to catch him. Then he'll be punished, properly according to law, and there won't be any consequences — except for him."

"What do you want?" Wu asked.

"I need information on jade — a lot of it. More important, all the available data on Mr. Wang's background: his other business activities, if any, his social life, his past. I need all this and more to track down the person who wanted him dead."

As he finished speaking another striking waitress appeared and replaced both drinks, despite the fact that Johnny's was untouched.

Johnny poured out a cup of coffee from the warming carafe and took a careful swallow. "Virgil, I won't hold out on you — I promise you that — but I don't have too much to give you. Wang Fu-sen lived very quietly, by himself until he took the Japanese girl in. If you want my guess on that, I'd call it pure charity and nothing else. The girl helped him and earned her keep, but not in bed. You may not understand this, not being Chinese, but he was a man of great dignity; not the pompous kind, but the real quiet inner kind that counts. He wouldn't take advantage of the girl for that reason alone."

Virgil remained quiet.

"Now maybe I can give you something you can use — I don't know," Johnny continued. "First I have to make a point clear. There are two entirely different attitudes concerning Chinese in this country. I consider myself a Chinese-American, in other words an American citizen of Chinese descent. So do almost all of us. But to the Chinese in China — Taiwan or the mainland — either way, we are overseas Chinese. Their feeling is that once Chinese always Chinese; they simply don't understand the concept of America — that both of us can be Americans despite our own heritages or the fact that the majority in this country are Caucasians."

He drank more coffee. "What this means, Virgil, is that the Chinese in the old country feel that they have a permanent hold on us and that we owe them our loyalty simply because our eyes slant — if they do. Understand that a lot of us do feel a close attachment to the real China — not the communist one — just as a lot of your young people go around sporting Afro hairdos." He buttered a breakfast roll.

"You are suggesting, then," Tibbs said, "that some people in China were applying pressure to Mr. Wang on the basis that he was Chinese — in their eyes. Was he a U.S. citizen, by the way?"

"Yes, he was. And your surmise is accurate, based on my own guesswork. I've had a little of that kind of thing and I expect that I'll get more. Most of it comes through Hong Kong; one letter I got I turned over to the FBI."

"That gives me an idea," Tibbs said. "I'll check to see if Mr. Wang ever took a similar step. Unless you know offhand."

Johnny shook his head. "I don't know, I can only guess."

"When can I see your jade collection?" Virgil asked.

"You really want to?"

"Yes, very much."

Johnny thought. "Why don't we just stay here and have some lunch. Then after that we can go over to my place — it isn't very far from here — and you can inspect my jades all you'd like."

"Could we skip the lunch?" Virgil asked. "I'm honestly not hungry. Unless you are."

Johnny took some more coffee. "Not really. I just thought that you might like the scenery around here. A lot more of it comes on duty at twelve. Unless a policeman can't admire pretty girls the way we do."

"If that were true, I wouldn't be a policeman," Tibbs said. "Invite me back some time; I'll buy the drinks."

"A deal. If you come down here much, why not become a member? I'll be glad to sponsor you."

"Many thanks, but I don't think I could handle the tab."

"It isn't that bad."

"All right, maybe later. When this matter is cleared away."

Johnny glanced up. "Am I under suspicion?" he asked.

"Let me put it this way: when I find the guilty man, I'll let you know."

Wu accepted that. "Let's go; I'm quite close by."

The jade collection of Johnny Wu was much more modest than the one in Wang Fu-sen's home, but its high quality was immediately evident. Furthermore, each choice piece had been carefully placed to display it to the best advantage. The lighting inside the three cabinets was artful: bright enough to illuminate, but subtle enough to flatter the stone objects at the same time. They needed no flattery; they were exquisite and Tibbs knew it.

"The longer I look at these things," he said, "the more I have to admire the men who created them. Perhaps for the first time, I wish that I had some prospect of being rich."

"Jade isn't cheap," Johnny admitted. "But consider

what goes into it. The stone comes for the most part from a small, very secluded section of Burma. It costs a great deal. After they get it and have it transported all the way to Peking, then the craftsmen are faced with one of the toughest and most intractable materials known to man. It takes weeks, and months, to turn out a good piece and the master carvers are dying out — they don't encourage them too much under the present regime. Do you know that they are actually making pieces now that show communist soldiers in battle and other propaganda subjects? It's a desecration; I've seen some in the commie department stores in Hong Kong."

When he had learned all that he could for the time being, Tibbs turned away from the cabinets. "Your collection is magnificent," he said.

"Thank you." Wu hesitated for a moment, then went on. "After a decent interval, I'm going to approach Miss Nagashima and see if she will sell me some of the pieces that Fu-sen had. You'll never find better in this country and there are a few things that I would like very much to own if I can get them."

Virgil looked at him. "Why Miss Nagashima?" he asked.

"I assumed that you knew. If you don't, you should. Fu-sen made a new will recently; in it he left almost everything he owned, including the jades, to her."

"Did he tell you that?"

"No, but word gets around. Chinese have always

been good at that. Do you want to leave that *Ya-Chang* with me for further study?"

"I think not," Virgil answered him. "It's evidence, so for the time being it should remain in police custody."

As Tibbs drove back to Pasadena certain ideas were forming in his mind, but they were too uncertain to be more than conjectures. There were elements missing and until they could be supplied, or accounted for, further development would be at the best slow and difficult.

He stopped at a coffee shop south of Colorado and had his usual lunch of a sandwich and a milk shake. He seldom varied this menu very much; the milk soothed his stomach and seemed to ease the tensions that went with his job. He could eat anywhere he chose now in the city, but there were still a very few establishments where he felt that his welcome was less than complete. He avoided them for the sake of the peace of his soul and allowed himself the luxury of eating where he knew that the color of his skin would have no bearing on his reception or how he was served.

After his meal he returned to his office for more paper work. There was no evading it and he had to keep up no matter what the cost in time and effort. Bob Nakamura was out on a bank holdup and this time there were no notes waiting on the desk. An hour later he made a phone call. Don Washburn was in his office and would be glad to see him if he cared to come to the plant.

As he drove north through streets Tibbs noticed how the mountains stood out in rare sharp relief; the air was remarkably clear and California looked as it probably had in the old Spanish days long before the internal combustion engine had been invented or oil refineries and power plants had been built to pollute the atmosphere.

At the gate that protected the research facility the formalities were at a minimum this time; he was expected. Once inside he was greeted by the receptionist and ushered almost at once to the large corner office where Washburn awaited him.

He had hardly seated himself before the trim executive secretary who had served him last time came in with two cups of coffee. This time she had not had to ask how he liked it; she supplied it, smiled, and withdrew.

"Mr. Washburn," Virgil began. "I'd like to ask you some very pointed questions if you don't mind. My purpose is to find the person who killed Wang Fu-sen. I know that you understand that."

"I do." Washburn looked as though he meant it.

"You told me that you had had some direct experience with narcotics in the case of your son Robin."

His host nodded. "Yes, that's true."

"How is he coming along, by the way?"

Washburn smiled. "Very well — he's returning home shortly."

"That's good news, certainly. Mr. Washburn, have you ever, at any time, known or suspected any connection between illicit narcotics and Mr. Wang? You mentioned that he was your close and good friend, and I'm making allowances for that."

Washburn was firm and decisive. "Absolutely not; I don't believe that he used them and I'm positive that he never trafficked in them. Let me give you a reason for that statement. I knew him for many years; for him to have dealt in dope of any kind would have been as out of character as a Salvation Army girl working in a bottomless bar."

Tibbs studied him before he put his next question. "Despite that endorsement, was there a possibility — and please note that word — that Robin might have been getting his supply of drugs from Mr. Wang? Please consider that carefully."

Apparently Washburn did. "Let me put it this way, Mr. Tibbs: Robin never met Wang Fu-sen to my knowledge except on one occasion when he came to our home for dinner. And perhaps not even then. I have a vague recollection that my boy was not home that night. Most certainly if they knew each other even casually, it was totally without my knowledge."

Virgil drank his coffee and changed the topic. "You confided in me the fact that you are doing research here for the Bureau of Narcotics and Dangerous

Drugs. I don't want to play games with you so let me put it directly: have you been working with keto-bedmidone?"

Washburn leaned back and drummed his fingertips against the top of his desk for a few seconds. "You couldn't have hit on that one all by yourself," he said finally. "So you must have been told. And by the Bureau. All right, the answer is yes. We've made some of the stuff here and it's been submitted to some tests. Even in the test lab, we lock it up in the safe overnight. And the people who work with it wear masks. It's pure hell."

Tibbs agreed. "I know that. What are its physical properties? In particular, what color is it?"

"White."

"A powder?"

"Tiny crystals."

"It's an injection drug?"

"Yes."

"Could a heroin addict use it in his usual manner?"

"Yes again. The heroin junkie could use his regular tools. If he did, God help him."

Virgil locked his fingers. "I want to ask you one more question that is vitally important. Please give me a candid answer; you know that I'll respect your confidence."

"I'll do my best."

"Mr. Washburn, do you have any knowledge, or well-founded suspicion, that keto-bedmidone may have appeared on the American market, particularly on the West Coast?"

Washburn more than took his time. "You are asking for highly confidential information, you know that."

"I do."

"You absolutely require it for your investigation?"

"I wouldn't have asked otherwise."

"Then I've got to accept your sincerity. As I told you before, I know who you are. Yes, Mr. Tibbs, it has appeared here and we're scared stiff."

"In Los Angeles?"

"Yes."

"When?"

Don Washburn moved in his chair in a way that showed his discomfort. His jaw worked slightly and his lips were hard together. When he spoke, his voice was matter-of-fact and unemotional, but only because he had made it that way. "A few months ago. And since you are sure to note it anyway, I might as well add that it began a very few days after the Japanese girl, Miss Nagashima I believe her name is, came to live in Mr. Wang's home."

CHAPTER 9

As soon as he was back once more in the spartan surroundings of his modest office, Tibbs sat down to do a piece of work that could wait no longer. From the top drawer of his desk he took out a small pad of paper, then he picked up a pen and began to write out notations. He put one on each slip of paper, using the green ink that he favored for this particular purpose. As he finished each one, he tore it off the pad and laid it aside. He kept at it until he had thirty-one individual memoranda written in his strong, precise hand.

When he had them all ready he cleared the top of his desk of everything else, took off his coat, and then began to lay out the small pieces of paper like an elaborate game of solitaire. Occasionally he shifted the positions of one or two of the paper slips; sometimes he spent a considerable time before he made up his mind where a particular memorandum would be placed. When he had all thirty-one of them down, it could be seen that they formed an irregular pattern, with several conspicuous gaps.

After the layout had been completed Virgil sat still, his hands in his lap, studying what he saw before him. He had an urge for a cigarette, but he had given that habit up long ago. He rubbed his chin with his right hand, then put it back into his lap. Twice he moved the position of one of the slips of paper. Otherwise the diagram he had prepared remained as it was, with open spaces where there were not enough data to fill them in.

It was approaching six in the evening when Tibbs had a visitor. He looked up to see the tall figure of Bob McGowan. "Am I interrupting you?" the police chief asked.

"No, of course not. Sit down."

McGowan eased himself down into one of the hard chairs. "I just wondered how things were going in the Wang murder. Do you see any light yet?"

Virgil motioned toward the display on the top of his desk. "I have some things; but there are too many gaps up to now. Actually there's a whole missing element, and until I can get hold of it, it's going to be rough."

"Would you like to have me assign you some help?"

"I don't think so, sir. I'm not being a prima donna: it's just that as of right now it's a one-man job. In a day or two it may be very different."

Bob McGowan crossed his long legs. "Is there a narcotics angle?" he asked.

Tibbs frowned. "Yes and no; I keep running into

strong suggestions, but nothing that I can pin down. If I had to bet I'd say that there's one somewhere, but there are contradictions too. For instance, everything that I've been able to get so far on the background of the deceased shows him to have been a man of exceptional character. And he was in more than comfortable financial circumstances — from legitimate activities."

"I understand that there's a young lady who was living in his home. Is she likely to be involved?"

At that moment Virgil was grateful for the color of his skin. He looked up with a poker face. "Right now I'd have to say that there's a very good chance of it, but I don't have anything definite on her either."

"That might be an angle to check a little more," McGowan said. "Why don't you spend some time with her, take her out to dinner."

Tibbs looked at his chief carefully, and read nothing in his features. "That's a good idea. I take it that it would be on my expense account?"

"I'll trust to your conscience, Virgil."

"Thank you. I won't overstep the bounds."

"I have complete confidence in you; I know you won't, not while the investigation is in progress." He reached across and pointed. "There seems to be a vacant space there. What goes in it?"

Tibbs allowed himself to smile. "That will be filled this evening, I hope. It's reserved for my opinion of Mr. Aaron Finegold's jade collection. I haven't seen it yet."

"Are you familiar with jade, Virgil?"

"No, sir, but I'm working on it."

The police chief got up. "Carry on. At least you can't complain about monotony. Nudist camps, kids with guns, baseball teams, exotic young ladies from the Orient . . ."

"Do you know what she is?" Tibbs asked quietly.

"She's a human being," McGowan answered. "That's enough for me."

"God bless you," Virgil responded.

Aaron Finegold met his visitor at the front door. "Good evening, Officer Tibbs," he said, "or is that the right title?"

"Let's skip the titles," Virgil suggested.

"Fine with me. Please come in. By the way, is this an official call or a social one?"

"I'd be pleased if you'd consider it both."

"In that case, the bar is open. Have you had your dinner?"

"Yes, thank you."

"Then how about joining us for coffee and dessert?"

"An imposition."

"Not at all. As a matter of fact my wife is interested in meeting you. She finished a book recently, something called *In the Heat of the Night*."

Virgil groaned. "Not that again, please. I'm trying to live it down."

Finegold led the way into a huge living room luxuriously carpeted with a deep-pile white rug. From a long, custom-made sofa a tall, graceful woman rose to greet him. "Miriam, this is Mr. Virgil Tibbs," Finegold said. "My wife."

"Good evening, Mr. Tibbs. Do sit down, please. We're about to have cake and coffee; in fact we've been waiting until you came."

"That's very kind of you."

"Not at all." As she finished speaking, a maid entered the room bearing a tray with individual portions of what appeared to be a tremendous chocolate cake made up of rich multiple layers. He was served with an oversized portion and given a sterling silver fork with which to eat it. When the coffee came it was provided in unusual cups which clearly had been imported from some designer's specialized collection.

"Now do tell me," his hostess invited, "are you here to arrest my husband?"

"No," Virgil answered her, "at least not until after I've finished my cake. I don't see this kind very often."

"We have it made especially," Finegold said. "I got the recipe in Zurich; they know how to do things with chocolate there."

For no visible reason the conversation stopped dead at that point. Tibbs ate his cake, which was almost too rich for his palate, and drank his coffee which was an unfamiliar kind, but excellent. He had almost finished before Miriam Finegold broke the silence. "I can't wait any longer," she confessed. "Please tell us why you came. I heard you tell my husband that this is partly an official call."

"Very well," Tibbs responded. "I came to ask permission to see your jade collection."

"You mean that — really?"

Virgil nodded. "I assure you that I do."

"By any chance," Finegold asked, "are any pieces missing from Mr. Wang's stock?"

"Not to my knowledge," Tibbs answered, "and if I'd come here on an errand like that, I wouldn't have eaten your cake first."

"There are times," Miriam Finegold said, "when my husband can't forget that he's a lawyer. I hope you don't mind too much."

The attorney got to his feet. "Let's look at the jade," he said.

There were seventeen pieces in the Finegold collection, all of them excellent. They were all miniature sculptures, of Chinese beauties, graceful animals, birds, and flowers. They varied in color; two of them were of a faint but clear lavender hue. Instead of being displayed together in a case, they were distributed about the jade room, so that the individual effect of each one was enhanced. They were all protected behind glass, but it was so artfully done that they seemed almost to be ready to be picked up and admired.

Tibbs turned to his hostess. "Is this your work?" he asked.

She smiled. "We did it together. We don't have too many pieces, but we like what we do have very much. Now that Mr. Wang is dead, I don't know whether we'll be adding any more or not. He seemed to give them a special aura of his own. He was a wonderful man."

"So I understand," Virgil said. "I know very little about jade, but I can appreciate beautiful things, and you certainly have a wonderful collection here."

After that he made the necessary small talk until he was able to excuse himself and return to his own car for the last trip of the day — back to his apartment.

Home at last he pulled off his shoes and flexed his weary feet. He had had a full day — too full. He mixed himself a drink, shed his coat, and took off his gun and holster. His handcuffs followed. Then he enjoyed the pure luxury of getting rid of his tie. He took a long pull at his drink and felt the alcohol coursing down his throat.

He turned on the reading lamp next to the most comfortable chair that he had, gathered up the two books on jade, and settled himself down to study.

He stayed there for more than three hours, taking occasional notes and learning some unusual things. When he finally rubbed his eyes and gave up for the day, he knew that jade was a whole culture in itself, one far out of the reach of a policeman's salary but fascinating nonetheless. He ate four cookies out of a box, drank a short glass of Seven-Up to slake his thirst, and went to bed.

In the morning nothing had gone away. None of the gaps in the layout he had made on the top of his desk had filled itself and the fact that the sun was shining did nothing to simplify his problems. He was eating breakfast when his phone rang.

He picked up the instrument and said, "Good morning."

"Good morning, Virgil, this is Frank Lonigan. How are you today?"

"Fine — I think. What's up?"

"Virgil, something has been developing here and we think that we ought to put you in the picture. It may or may not have a bearing on the case you're working on. Would you be free to have coffee with me in, say, half an hour?"

"Of course, why not. Where are you now?"

"Not too far away. How about Bob's near to the college?"

"All right; if it's too public we can talk in the car later."

"Good. See you there."

When the call had been completed, Virgil phoned the department to report when he could be expected. Then he finished dressing, rinsed off the dishes he had used, and left for his appointment.

Although he arrived two or three minutes early, Frank Lonigan was already there in a booth waiting for him. He rose to shake hands and then settled back down into the simulated leather upholstery.

When the order had been placed, Lonigan lit a cigarette and began talking. "Virgil, I've been in the narcotics control business for sixteen years, and I think that I know most of the answers. But lately there have been some developments that don't fit any pattern that I know. And while the connection isn't definite, it's entirely possible that they're related to the Wang murder."

"Don't stop now," Tibbs said.

"I won't. I don't know how familiar you are with our operation, but much of our work is overseas where we cooperate with Interpol and other police agencies to cut down the supplies at their source. Stopping illicit drugs at the border is the customs' responsibility; once they're inside, if they get here, then they fall under the jurisdiction of the local police authorities wherever they go and are marketed."

He stopped when the waitress arrived with coffee and sweet rolls.

"In this type of a setup, Virgil, we depend to a considerable degree on squealers — informers — who help us out, sometimes on a cash basis, sometimes for revenge or competitive reasons, and occasionally because they are responsible citizens who want to help. Therefore we make it a business to check out every tip that we get as long as it sounds at all reasonable. We've gone on a lot of wild-goose chases, but we've also bagged some important shipments. So in the long run it pays. Of course the information sources that we have set up ourselves are the most reliable and we have a good many people working undercover."

"I would expect so," Tibbs commented.

Lonigan broke a sweet roll and applied butter. "About five or six weeks ago we got a tip over the phone — anonymously — telling us about a certain shipment of merchandise that was coming up from Mexico. We got in touch with the customs people and alerted them. Without going into details, they intercepted sixty-three kilos of largely uncut heroin."

"Drugs are ordinarily off my beat," Tibbs said, "but that sounds to me like a mighty big bust. Approximately a hundred and forty pounds of heroin must be worth a tremendous amount of money — and it would probably supply the street traffic for months."

"Right in both cases, but that's not all." Lonigan ate more roll and washed it down with coffee. "This isn't an amateur business, you know. Whoever sent that heavy load of heroin up this way took his lumps and sent a replacement shipment by another route."

Virgil looked at him. "And you got a tip on that one too," he suggested.

"Right — from the same source as far as we can tell."

"The brotherhood will be looking for him — or her."

"That is certain. And I don't need to add that what I'm telling you is absolutely under the rose." He looked up as though he was not completely sure that Tibbs would know the reference.

"*Sub rosa* it is," Virgil agreed.

"Fine. With that understood, let me add a little more. We haven't been able to pin it down definitely, but we have been getting some input from the Far East that your murder victim was an importer of the stuff, in addition to his jade business."

Tibbs drank coffee and cleared his throat. "Frank, I know better than to dispute evidence, and I know too how people can put up a false front. But if Wang was in that business, he had every person I've met so far who knew him completely fooled. A number of very responsible citizens have been unqualified in their endorsement of him."

"Like that."

"Absolutely. Usually somewhere along the line, if anything is wrong, it'll come to light. Not this time."

Lonigan studied him. "Possibly it could be the girl," he said.

"Possibly," Tibbs agreed. "The time factor would be important there."

Lonigan emptied his coffee cup. "Here's why I want you in the picture, Virgil — I want to ask something. If you uncover any narcotics angle, or anything resembling one, in your investigation, please let me know. Immediately. It isn't just the usual thing."

"Meaning what?"

Frank Lonigan bent forward. "Virgil, put two things together and see what sort of a result you get. One: out of a clear sky we suddenly start getting tips that lead us to some of the biggest hauls in years. Two: we get the word that the Chicoms are trying to get keto into this country. And remember: not all narcotics addicts are street-corner bums. Some of them come pretty high up the social and economic ladder."

"Is there any evidence?"

"Yes, Virgil, there is. We've had four junkies DOA in the last two days. Three of them, according to our pathologist, had been hot-shotted — overdosed to death."

"What percentage of heroin does it take to do that?"

"Twenty-five or thirty, roughly — it depends on the addict and the purity of the drug. But these weren't heroin cases, Virgil. They died of keto-bedmidone."

When he got to his office Virgil was in no mood to talk to anyone. He hung his coat over the back of his chair, sat down, and noted a memo that Commander Reese of the LAPD had called him. That was getting up there; in the Los Angeles Police Department the commander rank was next above captain. He picked up the phone and returned the call.

The commander was brief, but potent. "I have the word that you have a problem with a possible narcotics angle. If the boys in room 321 can help you, count on us. And if you have any need to work in our jurisdiction, permission granted."

"Thank you, sir," Tibbs said. "As a matter of fact I was going to check with your narcotics people this afternoon."

"Good; I'll pass the word."

As he hung up the phone Virgil felt a little better. Things did not seem to be closing in on him quite so much. He knew where the gaps were in the layout he had made; it was a matter now of filling them. Including the one which did not show because it came at the very end — the name of the person who had done murder.

When he had gone through more paper work, and had disposed of those items which were the most pressing, he opened the telephone directory and began a patient job. There was an imposing list of stockbrokers and unless he got an unexpectedly good break, he would have to call them all. He began by checking the white pages and establishing that Mr. Harvey's Christian name was Elliot. That helped a little, since there was less likelihood of more than one active stock trader in the area with the same name.

On his sixth call he hit pay dirt. After he had identified himself to the branch manager's satisfaction, he was told that Mr. Elliot Harvey had a sizable account with the firm and a very active one. Any further information could not be given over the phone. That was a promising enough lead to send Tibbs across the street to where the official unmarked cars were parked in a neat tan-colored row. He took the one he had been assigned and was in the brokerage office within a few minutes.

When he had presented his credentials and satisfied the branch manager of the importance of his mission, he got the kind of cooperation he had hoped for. "Some of our clients are very secretive concerning their portfolios," the manager explained. "If you were concerned with one of them, I might have to ask you to produce an official request. Fortunately Mr. Harvey apparently doesn't care; he is a very direct and blunt person, but he has never instructed us to keep his account confidential."

"You are most helpful," Tibbs assured him. "I'd like to examine the records of his transactions for the past two years if I may. Perhaps you have an office somewhere that is out of sight where I can work."

"I think we can provide you with that. In the unlikely circumstance that Mr. Harvey should come in personally, what shall I tell him?"

"In that case, if you need the records simply come and get them from me. I know Mr. Harvey and I prefer for the time being that he not know of this visit."

"Very well. I think, Sergeant Tibbs — is that right? — that I am entitled to ask a question in return."

"I'll answer it if I can," Virgil said.

"Mr. Harvey is a margin customer and at times we have a considerable amount of money on loan to him. While it is nominally secured by his portfolio — I believe you see the direction of my concern."

"I do," Tibbs said. "At the present time I don't see any reason for you to be worried. Mr. Harvey is involved indirectly in a murder investigation; beyond that I can't go. And that information is not to be circulated."

"It will not be. I'll have my secretary show you to a vacant office; Mr. Fletcher isn't in today and you can use his. She will provide you with the records you need. I'd appreciate being kept informed as far as you are able."

"One more point," Tibbs said. "Do you know if Mr. Harvey also did business on a regular basis with any other broker?"

"I seriously doubt it. We've handled a considerable volume of transactions for him and in return we have given him a number of special services that he seems to appreciate."

"Thank you. I may be here for some time if you don't mind."

"All day if you like. If you need anything more, ask for me."

It did take much of the remainder of the day to accumulate all of the information that Virgil wanted. He worked patiently with a long yellow ruled pad, taking down data and making certain comparisons with the chart of the Dow Jones Industrial Average and the other major indicators. He worked straight through the lunch hour without being really aware of it, and completed his task a few minutes before three.

By that time the brokerage office was all but deserted; the 7:00 A.M. opening time of the market on the West Coast forced everyone to be in early, so few of the customers' men chose to remain very long in the afternoon. Weary, but contented, Tibbs straightened things up, put his own worksheets back into his briefcase, and returned the records of Elliot Harvey's account together with the other data he had borrowed.

The manager was on the point of leaving himself. "Did you get what you needed?" he asked.

"Yes, thank you. If anyone asks questions, I was one of the company's auditors. Do you have any Negro employees?"

"Oh yes, quite a few." The answer came back a little too hastily, but Virgil forgave him that; he had heard far worse in his lifetime. Apparently the manager realized it himself, for he tried to make amends. "It is entirely consistent that one of our auditors might be black. Many of our most important clients are black also."

Tibbs took the will for the deed, shook hands, and went back to where he had parked his official car. He did not especially care for the word "black": under no circumstances would he have referred to his office mate as "yellow." "Negro" and "Nisei" were dignified terms and he wondered how much longer it would take people, including his own, to learn to use them.

There was a ticket stuck under the windshield wiper of his car. Automatically he looked up and saw that he had been all day in a two-hour zone. He turned the slip of paper over to see who had been dumb enough to tag an official police car and found in red ink the words: *Naughty, naughty.*

That reminded him of the time that someone had put out over the official radio, "Do the crosstown buses run all night?" and without a moment's hesitation someone had come back, "Do-da, do-da!"

He checked the car back in and returned to his office. Bob was still out, presumably chasing bank robbers. If that were the case, the bandits in question had something to worry about. Bob Nakamura looked less like a police detective than any man on the force, which helped him to be one of the best in the business.

It was close to six when the phone on Virgil's desk rang. He picked it up, expecting an internal call, and said "Yes?"

He was slightly startled to recognize Yumeko's voice coming over the wire, "It is now I may still call you Virgil?" she asked.

"Of course. What can I do for you, Yumeko?"

"I have worry because of Chin."

"Chin? Who is Chin?"

"For three days he is gone," Yumeko said.

Tibbs reached for a pencil. "Now give me his full name and tell me who he is."

"He is Chin, Chin Soo. He is houseboy for Mr. Wang."

"Houseboy! No one told me about any houseboy."

"I am sorry. You did not ask and I did not think to say. He has gone away for three days."

It all came in a rush now, so much so that he hardly heard the words that continued to come over the wire. Houseboy! He should have thought of that, but as Yumeko said, he hadn't asked.

"I'll come over," he said almost mechanically, and then hung up. He was still a little dazed by the information. The missing element had turned up at last.

CHAPTER 10

Yumeko admitted him with concern plainly written on her face. Part of it was certainly for the missing house-boy, but it was likely that an equal amount reflected her worry that she had incurred Tibbs' decided dis-pleasure. "I am so sorry," she said before he could speak. "I did not tell; it was entirely my fault. I think so much about Mr. Wang that I forget Chin Soo!"

Then, to Tibbs' amazement, she held out her arms to him.

No gentleman could refuse that except under dras-tic circumstances. Virgil gathered her in and pillowed her head on his shoulder. He was acutely aware of the shaking of her body, of the acid tension that was rack-ing her. He had held girls in his arms before, but never one who was not completely of his own racial back-ground. He was not prejudiced, it was simply that he had never been able to shuck off the drastic inhibitions that had been implanted in him during his years as a boy in the Deep South. To him, at that moment, Yumeko was Japanese. The fact that half of her heritage was the same as his was subjugated and he remembered only that she had been born and raised in a foreign culture.

"Please, you will forgive me?" she asked.

For a moment he wondered if she were using her femininity to enlist his sympathy. Then he felt again the trembling of her body and knew that her question was genuine. "Of course," he said, and then forcefully held her at arm's length. He studied her as she looked up at him and he wished fervently, at that moment, that she was not involved in a murder investigation and one of the prime witnesses, if not a suspect, in the unhappy affair.

"I think that you'd better tell me all about it," he said.

Yumeko continued to look at him. "I have made a little food; will you sit and eat with me?"

He had forgotten about dinner. To accept would be another breach of police ethics and he knew it. "If you'd like," he answered. "But I want to know all about Chin Soo."

"Please to sit down." Yumeko gestured toward the living room. "It will be only a few minutes."

She came to the door after a scant five minutes and let him into the dining room. She had set two place mats and a small, intimate meal was waiting in basic

Japanese style — a number of different items each presented in a small bowl. There was no evident main dish as in Western dining. Tibbs sat down, unfolded his napkin on his lap, and recalled the time that he had prepared to have lunch in the kitchen of a converted farmhouse that served as the headquarters of a nudist resort.

A candle stood in the center of the table, but Yumeko did not light it. They helped themselves in silence for a few moments, then the girl began to explain. "When I come here Chin Soo was houseboy to Mr. Wang. I do not know how long he was here, but for a while anyway, because he did not act like he had newness. Mr. Wang spoke to him many times, always kindly, but Chin said little. I do not understand what they said, because they speak in Chinese."

"Chin was from the old country, then? I mean, he was not a Chinese-American."

"That is so, he was from Hong Kong, I think."

"Good. Go on."

"When Mr. Wang was made dead I have shock, I did not notice that Chin Soo was not here. His room is upstairs in the back of the house, so at night I never see him."

"One question. Did Chin Soo ever seem to be — fond of you?"

Yumeko lowered her eyes. "I do not think so. Mr. Wang did not encourage this and Chin Soo saw too clearly what I am."

For a little while it was quiet, then Yumeko continued. "I tell you now all that I know. Mr. Wang secured for me a position. I did not wish it, but it was his desire that I not live here all day, that I go outside and see people."

"I think he was right," Tibbs commented.

"Because it was his wish, I went; from the first day of work I came home to find . . ." She did not want to finish that sentence. "Chin was not here also, but that I did not think about. Then for a little while I think that he ran away because he was scared. But when he did not come back, then I called you on the telephone."

Virgil ate some spinach, which ordinarily he did not particularly care for, but the kind that Yumeko had fixed was delicious. "How old is Chin?" he asked.

"He has, maybe, twenty-five years."

"Is he tall?"

"No, you are more."

"Is he a strong man?"

"Not to be unusual. I do not think that he killed Mr. Wang with the knife, it would be too hard for him. Also Mr. Wang was very good to him. He was very good to everybody."

Tibbs was content to let things rest at that point for a little while; he finished his meal without again referring to either Mr. Wang or the missing houseboy. Instead he tried to put Yumeko at ease and at the same time to probe for anything that she might have forgotten to tell him. It was not until she had cleared away the food bowls and had brought in tea that he re-opened the principal subject. "Yumeko, did Mr. Wang ever say anything to you that suggested he might be facing trouble of some kind?"

"That is yes," she answered. "He said to me that there were evil spirits, but he did not mean that as it sounds, he meant that there were real things, things *like* evil spirits that were bothering him."

Virgil, now fully alerted, asked, "Did he say anything else, Yumeko?"

"He said also that the wind does not always blow out the candle, even if the flame is . . ." She could not find the word.

"Meaning that it was weak?"

"I think so."

"Feeble?"

"No."

"Faltering?"

"Yes, that is so! That is the word he said." She looked relieved that her language inadequacy had been overcome.

"Was he seeing a doctor?"

"I think not. He was old, but for a man of such age and small build, he was not weak — not faltering."

"It was something else then — something from out-side."

"I think yes."

"Have you any idea what it was?"

She shook her head. "I do not know. He never told me, and myself I see and hear nothing."

Ideas were beginning to form in Virgil's mind. "Yumeko," he said. "I want to ask a favor of you. Could we go into the jade room?"

She rose quickly. "Come, please. It is good that you are with me."

She led him into the rear of the house, unlocked the door with a key that was already in position, and turned on the lights. The chalked outline that had been on the carpeting was no longer there. Despite this last piece of cleanup, the presence of the former owner still seemed to hang in the air; Tibbs understood why Yumeko did not care to enter alone, and why she would probably continue to feel that way for some time to come.

"I'm trying to learn a little about jade," he said, "but the pictures in the books don't help a great deal."

She looked at him. "You like the jade?" she asked.

"Yes, I'm beginning to very much, but right now I want to learn certain things about it for another reason."

She understood. "I will help you. I myself do not know a great deal, but Mr. Wang is teaching me." She stopped abruptly and out of the corners of her expressive eyes twin tears began to roll down her cheeks.

Virgil stepped forward, folded his arms around her again, and patted her gently on the back, letting her recover herself while he remained quiet and waited. Even at that somewhat strained time he was intensely aware of her attractions. Then, reluctantly, he let her go.

It didn't make matters any easier when Yumeko looked up at him and said, "You are very good to me."

He swallowed and found his proper voice. "Explain to me about the jade."

Yumeko located the set of hidden keys and unlocked two of the cabinets. "In China they do marvelous work in many different stones," she explained. "Of these the best is jade, but also very good is rose quartz, rock crystal, lapis lazuli, and some others. There are also softer stones like serpentine and Bowmanite that are made into carvings; they look like jade but they are not real. Sometimes they are called 'new jade,' but it is not so."

"I understand that there are two kinds of jade."

"That is so, Virgil. Nephrite, it is real jade, for a long time it was the only jade. Then they find a new stone, also beautiful and very, very hard. It comes from Burma in a small place and is called now jadeite. I shall show you."

From one of the cabinets she had unlocked she took out an immensely complicated carving of a vase surrounded by entwined stems and flowers. It was all one piece, milky white in color. Quite casually she handed it to Tibbs, taking it off the small, carefully carved wooden stand which obviously had been made to hold it alone.

"Please to examine," she invited. "Do not make upside down, for the lid of the vase is loose and it is all hollow inside. This is very difficult to do. It is a real vase and it can be used as one. But it should not be done; it is too valuable for that."

Somewhat gingerly Virgil held the remarkable carving in his dark brown hands and studied it. The man who had made it had been a true artist as well as a master of the technique of working one of the hardest and toughest stones known to man. He could not begin to estimate how many weeks and months of patient labor it had taken to create this unquestioned work of art. He was in awe of it and understood without question why it was so expensive.

"It is not always that jade is green," Yumeko said. "It is found in almost every color, even black. The Chinese say that there are one hundred colors of white jade. That is mutton fat that you have — it is a very good kind."

When he had finished studying the valuable piece she took it from him and handed him another. It too was largely white, but there was also in the stone a suggestion of a very light and delicate green. The carving was of two Chinese women poling a boat; the wooden stand on which it fitted had been shaped to suggest waves and the texture of water. "This of the two sisters is jadeite," she explained. "It is harder than nephrite, rarer, and even more expensive. But it is also most beautiful. Do you have knife?"

"Yes," Tibbs said.

"Try to scratch it, you cannot. True jade is harder

than any steel, so no knife can make even a small mark."

Virgil studied the carving he held, one which had been done halfway around the world by a man whose name was unknown, since all jade carvings were anonymous. "Yumeko," he asked, "Do you have any funeral jades here?"

She looked at him, a little surprised that he was aware that such things existed. "Sometimes Mr. Wang had them, but not very often: he did not like. Jade for him was things beautiful; funeral jades are from tombs, sometimes made to bury with the dead for him to enjoy in the next world or to show his wealth, sometimes smaller ones to cover and fill the holes in the body."

"I'm studying about jade now," Tibbs said. "I will have to be careful or I will fall in love with it and I can't afford that."

"It is not always so expensive. Sometimes we have pieces for only maybe seven, eight hundred dollars. All are jade; sometimes people sent to Mr. Wang carvings that were very beautiful but not jade. He would not sell them except maybe to Mr. Wu who knew also that they were not real jade."

Virgil stayed for more than an hour, sensing that he was not wearing out his welcome, studying the many carvings that the room contained. He had not realized how many there were, they were so artfully displayed. He actually began to calculate if it would be at all possible for him to acquire a piece of his own someday, then he forced the thought out of his mind; jade was for those in the higher brackets and that was not a description which ordinarily applied to policemen, even top-ranking ones.

"Yumeko," he said when he was preparing to leave. "Did Mr. Wang import anything but the jades themselves? Was anything else packed with them?"

She shook her head. "His furniture, I think, it was made in Taiwan, but it came here many years ago. Otherwise he import nothing but jade. I think he have friends in many places in the Far East; they find for him real jades and send to him from places like Taipei, Singapore, and Bangkok. Never from Red China, for he did not like that place, even though it was his homeland."

That was interesting information if true. "You are sure about that?"

"Yes, very sure. Nothing ever comes in from the communist places: Mr. Wang would not buy pieces from the red people. Even though he had some of his own family people living in China, on the mainland."

Satisfied for the moment, Virgil thanked her once more for her hospitality and her help. Then he went to the door and, without lingering, took his departure. He drove straight to his apartment, let himself in, and then picked up his phone. After dialing he waited only a few seconds until Bob Nakamura answered. "Listen," Tibbs said, "I'm going into L.A.; I may be on to something. Feel like an evening on the town?"

"Why not. Where are you?"

"At home. Do you remember the outfit you wore when we staked out the bowling alley last month?"

"Right. Forty minutes OK?"

"Don't rush, we've got all night."

Virgil hung up and then walked thoughtfully into his bedroom. As he began to change his clothes he considered what he had learned that evening and how the pieces of the problem were beginning to fit together. From his closet he took out a pair of well-scuffed workingman's shoes, faded blue jeans, a shirt that had nothing left of its pride and only part of its original substance, and a worn cloth jacket that had never had more than minimum pretensions.

Carefully he laid aside the well-tailored suit that had cost him almost a week's pay and put his neatly shined shoes on the floor in the corner. He stripped down to his shorts and then put on the old trousers and the shirt, which was worn dangerously thin at the elbows. When he had completed his dressing he looked completely the part of a Negro laborer, and his manner began subtly to reflect his new role. His mind was no longer on the case for the moment: he was living again some of the days he had spent when the type of clothing he now wore represented the best that he had had. That had been many years ago, but their memory remained acute and he could never purge them completely from his mind. It was not acting, it was a regression to a seventeen-year-old who was only eleven years past the shock of discovering that he had been born a mutation of the majority who inhabited his country and that for the rest of his life he would remain one.

He mixed himself a whiskey and soda and drank it slowly, mapping his plans for the remainder of the evening and the night. He left the bottle out and set a fresh glass beside it to await his partner's arrival. Bob was not much of a drinking man, but tonight liquor on the breath was almost a necessity. Or if not that, at least very much in character. He felt better after the highball and made himself another; he was just finishing it when the doorbell rang.

Bob Nakamura presented a different picture. There were few Japanese-Americans who ever appeared disreputable, but many of them earned a living from the soil and dressed accordingly. The transformation in Bob's case even included grime under his fingernails and a faint odor of perspiration which clung to his garments. "What's on the program?" he asked.

"The narcotics beat, but we're not out to make buys. I want to know what's going on. If we have to buy, we do, but we're not after the pushers. Actually I don't think that there's too much junk around."

"I've heard too that it's tight. Anything else?"

"Yes." Virgil motioned toward the makings of a highball. "Help yourself. This is to go no farther, but there may be a new drug out on the street. Something particularly dangerous. Even worse than horse."

Nakamura looked up, bottle in hand. "*Worse* than heroin?"

Tibbs nodded. "A synthetic, leave it at that. Just

don't take any; don't even sniff it if we run across some."

Bob looked at him. "Virg, do you realize what you're saying?"

"Yes, I do. There's strong evidence that it's connected with the case I'm on."

"Is it addictive?"

"Extremely so."

Nakamura dropped into a chair. "Good Lord."

Virgil lifted his own glass. "Now you know what we're up against."

Bob thought for a few moments. "Does LAPD know?"

"I presume so — the Bureau will have put them in the picture."

"Was your Mr. Wang peddling this stuff?"

"That's one of the things I'm trying to find out. When you're ready, we'll start."

"Two minutes, I need this drink now. I brought a car, incidentally, in case you need one in character. I picked it up from the dealer lot; it's a nine-year-old Chevy, but it runs better than it looks."

"Good." Tibbs picked up the phone again and called the night-watch supervisor at police headquarters. "This is Virgil," he reported. "Bob Nakamura and I are going into town. Would you advise the LAPD that we're coming into their jurisdiction? We expect to be on the street most of the night. We're going to 1212 South Alvarado, after that to the Central Market area and then South Central."

"Will do. Do you expect to need any help?"

"If we do, we'll ask for it."

"Do that. I'll pass the word to room 321 — it is narcotics you're on, isn't it?"

"Right." Virgil hung up.

"By the way," Bob asked, "why are we together?"

"We're in love," Tibbs answered.

"I always did think that you were kind of cute."

Virgil aimed a mock kick at him and then set down his glass. Together they left the apartment, climbed into the ancient car that Bob had borrowed, and headed toward the freeway.

After passing the four-level intersection Bob continued to head south on the Harbor Freeway until he reached Olympic. There he turned off and headed west, past the headquarters of the All-America Karate Federation which Virgil knew so well, and on to Alvarado where he turned south.

The California state facility for paroled narcotics offenders had once been a motel; it still looked so like one that hardly a night went by without someone driving in looking for accommodations. What had been the guest rooms were now occupied by men, three or more to a unit, who were free to accept employment during the daytime and who paid a minimum price for their beds and food. Many of them had long histories of addiction; several had been through the agonies of withdrawal many times. What there was to be known about the narcotics scene was likely to be known there.

When Tibbs and Nakamura arrived they were expected; one of the parole officers was waiting for them. "What can I do for you, gentlemen?" he asked. He knew who they were and the appearance they made had no effect on him.

"I'm on a murder investigation," Virgil told him. "It has a narcotics angle, but we're not out to burn anyone for that, not this trip anyway. I need information."

"Billy Lester might be able to help you."

"How do you want to work it?" Bob asked.

"Go on into the office, I'll send for him."

Some five minutes later Billy Lester appeared. He proved to be a tall, rangy Negro, well past fifty and sporting a trimmed beard which had a suggestion about it of a Spanish cavalier. He came in and seated himself, completely at his ease. "Boss man tells me you kinda want to know what's goin' on," he said.

"That's right," Tibbs acknowledged. "We're not out for the pushers or the junkies this time round. It's something bigger."

"You after the importer hisself?"

Bob Nakamura shook his head. "Murder," he said. Lester understood perfectly; explanations ended at that point.

"What you want?" he asked.

Tibbs walked over to the soda machine, fed in coins, and extracted three drinks. He passed them around and then took a long pull of orange before he answered. "We'd like to know how things are."

Lester crossed his feet. "Man, they ain't good. You ain't heard?"

"No, tell us," Virgil invited.

"Well, all of a sudden the junk — it's gone. Just a little bit left. When it's used up, if no more comes in, then the panic's on. You know what that means — no junk anywhere. That's when the junkies start hitting the drugstores, looking for doctors' cars, and go for paper. Some of 'em are pretty cute when it comes to faking symptoms so's they can get a prescription. But if they make it, it's only one fix. A lot of 'em will hit the hospitals if it gets really bad; put in for the cure. Anything but cold turkey: man, that's hell!"

"Maybe you haven't heard," Bob said. "There was a big bust late this afternoon — about six. Down toward Watts. They got more than five kilos, in bulk."

Lester looked startled. "Man, that's bad news! I'm off the stuff myself, but that was probably the last stock in town. It's gonna be bad, real bad." He shook his head.

"Billy," Virgil said, "you heard, didn't you, that four junkies were DOA in two days?"

"Sure, I heard. Some say they got hot-shotted — the stuff was too good and they went out right there."

"In one case that was probably it," Tibbs told him. "The other three were different."

Lester finished his drink and set the bottle down. Then he leaned forward and spoke more softly. "I know what you mean, the word's out. It was the new stuff, wasn't it?"

Virgil nodded. "I think so."

"I told 'em," Billy continued, "but that's the trouble with junkies — let something new come along and some of 'em's gonna try it just to be sure they ain't missin' nothin'."

"Like fruit salad," Tibbs suggested.

"Yeah, that's it, mix up all the pills in a bowl and then everybody take two or three just to see what you get. Some awful funny things come out of that. But the new stuff, man I don't want none of that."

"What's the word?" Bob asked.

Lester didn't hesitate to answer. "If you get it right, man, you fly — higher than anything else that's ever been. I know a couple guys who tried it. They're just living till they can get some more again."

"Think it's going to catch on?" Virgil asked.

Lester stared at him. "What do you think, man — course it is! Some junkies, they don't care what happens so long as they get that big lift. And with the new stuff they're really in the sky. I ain't never had none, but they say it's like the first time all over again, only bigger and better."

"I'll give it to you straight," Tibbs said. "We know what it is. If you get hooked on it, there's no out. Then, if there isn't any more, God help you."

Slowly Lester inclined his head. "I hear you talkin'. I been there and I don't wanna go back. I've fixed once in a while, but the steady stuff is out."

Virgil knew that the chances of that being true were limited, but it wasn't his immediate concern. "Thanks," he said to Lester, and shook hands. Then he nodded to Bob and together they went back to the borrowed car.

"Where to?" Nakamura asked.

"Let's try the Central Market. If we can't hit there, then we'll pretty much know what the score is."

"Do we buy?"

"Yes, if we have to. I've got some funds. If they offer us any of the 'new stuff,' we buy that too."

Bob started the car, drove out, and headed north. "Do you want to fill me in?" he asked.

"You've got most of it already. The main item is that the new narcotic seems to be pretty closely tied in with the Chinese gentleman who got himself killed on my beat. The problem is: everyone that I've talked to has given him tops marks for sterling character."

" 'For ways that are dark and tricks that are vain, the heathen Chinee is peculiar,' " Nakamura quoted. "There's some limited truth in it, despite the fact that it's as racist as hell. He could have conned everybody."

"By a lengthy process of incredible logic and almost inhuman deduction, I was able to reach the same conclusion," Tibbs said. "Incidentally, his houseboy's disappeared."

"Well that could be it! . . . I'm sorry, I've been like this all day. Is anybody looking for the houseboy?"

"We are — among other things."

"I think I see a faint glimmer of light." Nakamura

kept quiet while he threaded his way northward through the downtown and the largely Spanish area where the block-long Central Market was located. There he parked the car, not too difficult at that hour, locked up, and joined Virgil on the sidewalk. "You call the signals," he said.

"How many people can tell the difference between Chinese and Japanese?" Tibbs asked.

"Damn few, particularly among the Caucasians."

"All right, the missing houseboy, whose name is Chin Soo, is your cousin. Not brother, somebody might know better, but cousin is hard to dispute. That gives us a legitimate reason to be interested in him."

"And why do we think that he might be down here?"

"Because he may be involved in the dope flow that seems to be centered about Wang's home. The old man could have been involved himself, but there are some reasons to doubt that. That leaves two possibilities, the girl Yumeko and Chin Soo. Chin took a powder three days ago."

"I can see why it would be very interesting to interview my young cousin. Have you any angles?"

"Yes, but first things first. I want to find out what the scene is."

Together they began to drift, looking into the coffee and doughnut stands, apparently window-shopping even where the stores were closed. Gradually they made their way eastward south of the Little Tokyo area, working toward Main Street and its missions, sex-oriented theaters, and hock shops. In this environment Virgil let his shoulders droop slightly forward and moved his feet with a suggestion of a shuffle. Bob Nakamura was more self-effacing, as though he had not been in the country too long and was still slightly afraid of his environment. Many times, when they encountered someone alone who appeared to be on the street like themselves, Tibbs asked if he could make a connection. When he did, his speech intentionally reverted to the black English of his boyhood; the *r*'s disappeared and the heavy slur that it had cost him so much work to eradicate returned like a mother tongue. He knew that the typical Negro speech of the South marked the black man more surely even than the color of his skin. Those who got rid of it usually prospered; those who could not were assumed by the Caucasian majority to be lacking in intelligence, whether they said so or not.

His appearance, his manner, and his speech made him simply another Negro on the street, seconded by a slightly confused Japanese who was probably a homosexual. And they were addicts, as well they might be. But every time they found what might have been the right man, they got only a shake of the head.

While Virgil carried on alone, probing into the alleys and the dark entryways, Bob walked the several blocks back and retrieved the car. In it they drove south, down Central Avenue into the completely black area marked by a wide mixture of businesses, nude bars, vacant storefronts plastered with obsolete election posters, and billboards which flashed the smiles of Negro models and celebrities promoting products and services.

On foot once more, and shadowed by his apparently docile partner, Virgil tried to make contact with the retail narcotics market. Ordinarily it would not have taken him too long; the Los Angeles Police Department was seriously understaffed in its narcotics division and without the additional manpower that it needed, it faced an almost superhuman task. A high priority went to the school campuses where addictions were spawned, but even that vital function was curtailed by lack of funds. But the lack of adequate surveillance in itself could not account for the almost total absence of any of the usual traffic on the streets. Time after time Tibbs tried, but whenever he made his approach, he received nothing back but silence and sometimes blank stares.

"How much longer are we going to keep trying?" Bob enquired.

"Until I get something specific; I knew it was going to be tough."

"Just wanted to know," Bob said. "I can stay with it as long as you can."

At the end of the block they were on was a closed theater; when they reached it just beyond they found a small knot of young blacks whose business, whatever it was, was their own. When Virgil saw them he did not hesitate. While Bob appropriately hung back, he walked up slowly, knowing that he would stop whatever conversation was going on. Silence greeted him as he joined the circle.

He looked around the group, apparently a little bit in discomfort, and then asked, "Hey, where kin I make a hit? I gotta get it real bad."

No mimic could have done it — the difference would have been apparent to those who listened — but by his voice, more than anything else, he convinced them. Not all, perhaps, but one lanky youth of about twenty answered him. "Man, where you been?"

"Travelin'," Tibbs answered with proper vagueness. "We got in little while ago. I need it, man, he'p me!"

Again he was subject to casual but intense scrutiny. Then one of the group nodded toward Bob. "Who dat man?" he asked.

"He's ma frien'," Virgil let his eyes flutter slightly as he said it and they read him.

"He don' belong here," someone said.

Tibbs responded properly; he drew himself up a little, but not too much, and repeated, "He's ma frien'."

The lanky young man took over. "You in trouble, man, deep trouble. You ain't heard. They ain't nothin', nothin' at all."

Virgil's eyes searched in different directions, as though they could seek out a reprieve from that statement. "They's always some," he protested. "Ain't nevah dried up."

With a casual movement of his hand the youth invited him to follow. Virgil did so as Bob, apparently hesitantly, tagged along well behind. Walking with almost maddening slowness the young Negro led them behind the theater and down an alley. Tibbs was unafraid; he sensed that he had been accepted on short acquaintance and if the party got rough, he could take care of himself. Bob too was far more qualified than his somewhat dumpy figure suggested. Neither of them was armed; the clothing that they wore was not suitable for concealing any kind of an adequate weapon.

Their guide apparently was unconcerned about who they might be; he led the way farther down the alley and then stopped before a small detached garage. It was a clapboard affair, built to minimum standards behind a house that was steeped in neglect. It had once been painted, but the color was so far gone it had faded into nothingness. The tall youth pulled open one side of the split door and pointed inside.

The floor was covered with dirt and ancient leaves. In the corners some worthless items had been haphazardly stored. But the thing which demanded attention was the man lying, face down, in the litter. He was clothed in an old pair of jeans and a shirt which he had half torn off his body. If he was even aware that the door had been opened, he gave no visible sign. His body was steadily rolling back and forth, interrupted only when he kicked his legs violently as though some unseen creature was trying to seize them in its jaws. His hands were across his face, protecting it in part from the debris in which it was all but buried. As he ceaselessly rolled and twitched, he kept up a constant, chilling series of subdued cries and moans. As Virgil watched he turned over and began to roll on his back, revealing the mask of sweat that covered his face. His eyes were alternately wide open and squeezed tight shut, as though they too shared the agony that racked his body. His rolling, twisting movements never ceased as his body fought to find some nonexistent position which would offer it a modicum of relief.

"You know what dat is?"

"I know," Tibbs answered. "Cold turkey. Man, he needs stuff awful bad."

"Yeah," the man who had brought him answered. "I know. He's my frien', and I ain't got nothin' to give him. So he's got to take it, like mebbe you too by tomarra'. So if'n I ain't got none for him, what for you?" Then he fell silent and watched his friend, aware of his unanswerable argument.

"Mebbe a doctor?" Virgil suggested.

His guide shook his head. "He can't take another bust. The Feds, they doin' it to him 'cause they grabbed all the stuff." The seeming injustice of that caused him to tighten his thick lips and for a moment his fists clenched.

"If'n I had some junk, I'd give it to him," Tibbs said.

The lanky youth shut the door, consigning the man

inside to his fate. "He ain't the only one. All over town. You know what a panic is?"

"No junk."

"Yeah, no junk. Well, man, we got us a panic. There ain't nothin', so you're shit outa luck. Unless you want to try the new stuff; that might help ya."

Virgil rolled his eyes wonderingly. "What dat?" he asked.

They emerged back onto the street once more. "I dunno, it's sumthin'. Ya might get hot-shotted; ya gotta take a chance."

Tibbs grabbed him as though in mild desperation. "I wan' it," he said, "I wan' it bad! Where kin I get it?"

The youth shook his head. "You gotta find the Chinamen," he answered. "They got it."

"An' what's it called? I gotta know that!"

The young man shook himself loose. "Jus' ask for jade dust," he answered.

CHAPTER 11

On the way back to the car Virgil was strangely silent; his hands were thrust into the pockets of his disreputable jacket and he walked with his head down, deep in his own thoughts. After an interval Bob asked, "Can we help him?"

"Not really," Tibbs answered. "He's having it damn tough, but unless he has a bad heart condition or something like that, he's in no danger. What treatment facilities there are will be overloaded already: it's not as though we were denying him something."

"And, of course, if we do pass the word we'll both be dead on the street for months to come."

"Years, probably," Virgil said. "We can't afford it. That's the main consideration, of course." He stopped and looked as far as he could in both directions. "The panic's on, no doubt about that. That means that there are, or will be, hundreds more like him hidden away somewhere to go through their agonies, and more who are still on their feet out trying to make a buy somewhere. They'll put up the last thing they own for any kind of a bag at all."

"I know," Bob agreed. "I had one a few weeks back — heroin addiction in an eleven-year-old girl. A boy gave it to her — he was fifteen."

Virgil reached the car and unlocked it. "The hell of this damn business is that the public has no idea what goes on and wouldn't believe it if they were told. Let's go home."

He climbed in and seated himself behind the wheel. Bob noted how his lips were pressed together and understood — as he had many times in the past. He got in without comment and was glad when the vehicle began to move. The area was fearfully depressing to him and the image of the man fighting pain on the floor of the dirty garage would not get out of his mind.

Two blocks farther on Virgil stopped for a light. While they waited for it to change Bob noticed two men talking together in a darkened doorway; the one who was facing toward the street was shaking his head; then he held his hands out expressively to show nothing. The light came green and they moved forward once more. The car accelerated up to the legal speed; then Virgil began to apply the brake. Bob looked back quickly and saw the red lights on the patrol car that was behind them. That meant another two or three minutes shot to hell. Normally he was not impatient, but the neighborhood was beginning to get him down and he wanted to get it behind him and out of his sight if not his mind.

Obediently Tibbs pulled over and stopped. The cruiser drew up behind him and both of the uniformed men it contained got out, fitting on their caps as they did so. Bob knew exactly what to expect and he was not disappointed — one of them came up to talk to Tibbs while the other came up on the right and opened the car door. "Would you get out please, sir," he said, and motioned with a flashlight he held in his hand.

Bob drew breath, but then for the moment decided to hold his peace. This was Virgil's party and he was willing to let his partner call the signals. Just to make things interesting he deliberately swayed a little when he got to his feet and managed to look properly confused. The officer spoke to him again. "Will you step over here, please, sir." Just before he moved out of hearing range he caught Virgil's heavily accented speech, "Ah ain't done nuthin' mister, what-cha wan' me for?"

Since that was the way it was to go, Bob gladly played along. As he walked he managed almost to trip himself and then stood waiting. Promptly the officer pulled a card out of his pocket and began to read. "I am about to give you a sobriety test, but before I do so I will inform you of your rights. Do you understand me?"

When he required it Bob could produce a Japanese accent in any one of several expert variations. He nodded his head a little uncertainly and then said, "Speak most slowly, please."

In response the uniformed man read from the card, pronouncing each word as carefully as he was able. As a result he overpronounced and Bob was, behind his wooden face, duly amused. But not a vestige of it appeared externally. Then Bob was asked to stand with his feet together, to hold out his arms horizontally, and then to touch the tip of his nose with his right forefinger. It took him some seconds of apparent motor difficulty to get into the required position; after that he brought his right arm in and tapped his nose with careful precision.

Next he walked down a crack in the sidewalk on request, fumbling his way into position and then performing with maddening correctness for the specified distance.

The officer led him back to the car. There his partner was carefully interviewing Tibbs and had read him his rights as well. "I want to ask your cooperation," he was explaining. "I would like to have your permission to look through your car."

"Ain't nuthin' wrong with ma cah," Virgil responded, and then visibly brushed imaginary perspiration from his forehead.

"I'm sure there isn't, but may I look at it anyway?"

"If'n yah sure, what-cha wan' to look at it fo'?"

"Let's just say that I'm curious."

Tibbs shrugged. "OK, then."

The search occupied the next five to ten minutes. At the end of that time the man who had been interviewing Tibbs finally looked up satisfied. "Thank you for your cooperation," he said, trying to conceal a certain disappointment.

"That's quite all right," Virgil told him. "We don't mind in the least. And you did search very well. Next time check up under the dash and don't forget the undersides of the fenders as well. That's a hiding place that's been used quite a bit lately."

The officer straightened up and looked at him. "What did you say that your name was?"

"I don't recall that you asked me."

"All right, I'll ask — what is your name?"

"Tibbs."

"And where are you from, Mr. Tibbs?"

"Pasadena."

"I see." He took his time, several seconds of it, quite deliberately. "That would be Mr. Virgil Tibbs, I take it."

"Remarkable," Tibbs said. "You amaze me."

"I go to the movies sometimes. I seem to recall, though, that you were supposed to be from Philadelphia."

"No way."

The officer relaxed. "OK, it's on us — we get days like this every now and then."

Virgil laughed. He let his head go back, and some of the tension that had been building up for hours ebbed out of him. "We're buying the coffee," he said, "if there's a decent place where we won't be spotted."

"There is, Virgil, believe it or not. It's a couple of miles; follow us."

The all-night stand was the ultimate in unsophistication, but the coffee was hot and excellent. The pastry was fresh and better than would be expected, so for the next half hour the four men sat together and exchanged shop talk. "Why did you stop us?" Bob asked.

"We saw you while you were waiting for the light. We've had the word that there's a highly dangerous new narcotic out on the street and to stop it at all costs. The only information we have to go on is that the distributor is supposed to be a Chinese. So considering the hour and the location, you looked like a good prospect."

Bob nodded. "You were alert. When I heard them talking about Chinamen, I wondered if I might get elected somewhere along the line. Not everyone can tell the difference — very few, as a matter of fact."

One of the uniformed officers stood up. "We've got to get back to work," he said. "It's a bad night; several drugstores have been broken into and four or five doctors' offices have been hit. It's going to get worse."

Presently the two cars pulled away from the all-night restaurant: the patrol car to go back into the Central Avenue district, the ancient Chevrolet to return up the freeway into Pasadena. "Virgil," Bob asked, when they were well on their way, "do you see any light in this thing at all?"

"Some," Tibbs replied. "I got one idea tonight that may lead to something. We didn't waste our time — and thanks for your help."

"I didn't do anything."

"Oh yes you did; if I'd been alone it would have been a different story." He lapsed into silence then and remained that way until Bob dropped him off in front of his apartment. He was bone tired by then, too tired to even think anymore. He undressed, stored his work clothes in a corner of his closet, and contemplated a shower to wash off the last traces of the area where they had been. He was too exhausted even for that, instead he crawled into bed and yielded immediately to sleep.

When he awoke his mood had changed. Frustration was beginning to eat away at his composure; he felt strongly that his progress was too slow. After breakfast he set out to interview all of the neighbors of the late Mr. Wang.

His first six calls were nonproductive. Experience had taught him that in work of that kind it was necessary for him to identify himself immediately, otherwise the reactions he got were usually hostile. It was not particularly because of his color; the plethora of door-to-door salesmen who kept the homeowners of Pasadena under steady attack had built up a determined resistance to any kind of unexpected callers. At each of the six houses he had been accepted as a police officer after he had produced his credentials, but at only two of them was he invited inside. One housewife had kept him standing during the interview, but the other not only asked him to sit down, but also offered him tea.

"Our home was robbed a little over a year ago," she explained, "and your people were so helpful. And Mr. Thistle, I still remember his name, he caught the man who did it and got back our color TV for us. So anything I can do to help, please just ask me."

Despite her willingness, she had nothing to offer that was pertinent. She told how the neighborhood had been upset when "a Chinaman" had moved in, and how that feeling had dissipated when it had become evident that nothing was going to go to rack and ruin as a result. She herself had never met the man, but he had a reputation for very quiet living and impeccable conduct. She knew about Yumeko, but had assumed along with everyone else, apparently, that she was his daughter. It had helped that the few callers that Mr. Wang had been observed receiving had all been Caucasians, which dispelled the suspicion that an opium den was operating in the area. Virgil finished his tea, thanked her, and continued his rounds.

Just before lunch he had his first tangible result; the woman who received him apparently was glad to have someone to talk to. Unlike the others whom Tibbs had interviewed, she had not reconciled herself to having an Oriental for a neighbor. "I can't say anything against him really," she declared, "but of course you know how they are — not being white people and all that." She hesitated. "I'm sorry if I offended you, but you do know — of course. Well, a while ago that girl went to live with him. She's a strange one, never shows her face and keeps the draperies closed all the time. I don't know what goes on in there, but I'm not surprised that you're asking. And these Chinamen coming and going all the time."

"How many Oriental people were there altogether?" Tibbs asked.

"Well, there was the old man himself, the girl of course, and there was a boy — a servant, I expect. He went to the supermarket all the time — I've seen him buying food there. But there were others. I saw two Chinamen going in there not many days ago."

"Could you describe them?"

"Who can describe Chinamen! Just two of them, that's all. They had on business suits and came together, that's all I can tell you."

"Did you happen to notice what kind of a car they were driving?"

"Well, yes — it was a new car and light-colored. I don't know what brand it was, they all look so much alike nowadays."

"One more thing," Tibbs said. "Since you are very

observant, you might have noticed this. Was either of
the men carrying anything when they went into the
house — or when they came out? Say a box, for
example."

She shook her head. "I'm quite certain that they
didn't take anything in or out. One of them might have
had a briefcase or something like that, but nothing
bigger. I just happened to be looking out of my window, to see if the postman was coming, when I saw
them."

When he was satisfied that there was nothing more
to be learned for the moment, Virgil thanked her and
left. He made five more calls after that and on one of
them obtained confirmation of the two Chinese who
had been seen calling on Mr. Wang. Despite this, the
finding was not too significant, in fact it was more than
reasonable that Mr. Wang would have had Chinese
callers from time to time. He went back to his office
with the feeling that while he had not learned very
much, at least he had disposed of an obvious duty and
one which was part of a great many investigative pro-
cedures.

In the early afternoon he was back in court once
more to give evidence; he sat there for almost three
hours and was not called to the stand. When he finally
got away, the day was effectively gone. It didn't help
matters when he found on his return that a fresh pile
of paper work had been left on his desk. He wrestled
with it until it was well past quitting time and then,

emancipated at last, he went out, got into his car, and went home.

The only work he did that night was to call briefly on Donald Washburn and ask to see his jade collection. Once more he was politely received; he viewed a display of about twenty pieces of varying quality from good to superb and expressed his appreciation of them.

"Not all of them are what they should be," Washburn told him. "When I started out collecting I didn't know too much about jade and consequently I got stuck a few times. Not badly, but a few of my pieces are imitation, I know that now. Someday I'm going to clean them all out and have nothing but real jade and fine carvings. Francis Wang was going to help me with that, but of course he can't now."

"Is your son back yet?" Tibbs asked.

"Yes, he is, and we're most happy about it, of course. He's out right now, looking up some of his friends — not the wrong ones, I assure you."

Virgil turned to go. "Thank you very much for your time. I don't want to intrude on you any more than is necessary."

"You're quite welcome anytime, professionally or socially. If you want to talk to Robin for any reason, I'll set it up for you."

"That's very kind. I don't have any need at present, but I may want to talk to you again later."

"Fine, just let me know."

With that out of the way Tibbs went back to his apartment, kicked off his shoes, and stretched out with a drink. He lay full length on his davenport, his glass in his hand, and thought about Yumeko. She had a certain spunk that he admired very much, even though he felt that she was oversensitive about her heritage and mixed bloodstream. It was a sign of the future, her origin that was, a forecast of the day when people simply would be people.

He refilled his glass, and then settled down to study once more. He picked up the *Chinese Jade Throughout the Ages* and returned to his perusal of the Han Dynasty.

When he had been at that more than an hour his attention began to flag; it was heavy reading and he had had a tiring day. Rather than give up he began to turn the pages, looking at the color plates of some of the world's most distinguished jades and comparing them in his mind with those he had seen at the Wang house and in the several private collections he had already viewed. He remembered the variety of colors, the many different types of carvings, and the almost inhuman ingenuity that had been used in working some of the rare stones.

Then, at that moment, he saw it. He stopped with a breath half drawn and then involuntarily opened his mouth as the pieces he had gathered, abruptly and without warning, fitted themselves together. He had worked some things out by a process of hard thought, but the big one had been in front of him all the time and he had not seen it. He had been stupid, stupid and blind as a bat! His telephone was right beside him: he picked it up and called the department.

"This is Virgil," he said. "There's been a development. I don't want to go into it now, but I want an immediate watch put over the Wang house — front and rear. Set up a stakeout and keep it on. Do you have the address?"

"Right, Virg," came back from the night desk man. "How soon do you expect action?"

"Anytime, we may have missed it already. I don't think so, but set it up as quickly as you can."

"Will do. What are the boys to look for?"

"Any and all comings and goings. Let the girl who lives there go out and in undisturbed. Also there's a houseboy — a Chinese about twenty-five or so; if he shows, all right, but let me know immediately. I'm at home. Anybody else, anybody at all, call me right away."

"Anything else, Virg?"

"Yes — don't intercept any normal traffic in or out of the house, but don't let anyone carry anything out, no package no matter how small. If anyone attempts that, stop them and use any excuse until I can get there."

"What have you got, Virg?"

"As soon as I can prove it," Tibbs answered, "I've got myself a murderer."

CHAPTER 12

For much of the night Tibbs tossed and turned. He was entirely confident that the watch over the Wang house was in effect and would take care of any sudden contingencies, but the sharp images that were in his mind would not relent and let him get any sleep. He contemplated taking a phenobarbital, but rejected the idea because he might have need to be acutely alert at any time and he could not risk it. Remembering what he had learned in the Aikido *dojo*, he tried consciously to relax his tensions and let his thoughts compose themselves, but when he began to feel that he was making some progress, his pillow conspired to become hot and lumpy and the bedclothes trapped his legs in their folds.

He got up even earlier than usual and made himself some strong black coffee. He followed it with orange juice and felt a twinge of acid stomach as a result. He shook a small amount of baking soda into a glass, added water, and drank it down. Then, unable to restrain himself any longer, he called in and asked what had happened during the night.

Everything had been quiet at the Wang house; the stakeout had been in full effect, but the report was entirely negative. Business had been dull.

He looked at the clock and wondered if it was too early to call Yumeko. He had no idea when she got up to go to work, but she was employed in Little Tokyo and would have to allow at least forty-five minutes' travel time to get into Central Los Angeles. Assuming that she started at nine, she would have to be up at least by seven-thirty. He waited an impatient twenty minutes and then dialed the number.

He felt a hot flush of gratitude when her voice came on the line; it gave some evidence of interrupted sleep, but there was no petulance in it. "What time do you leave for work?" he asked.

"It does not make any work today, Virgil, because it is Saturday."

He had completely lost track of the days of the week.

"Are you going to be home today?"

"If it is your wish, I will be here. For a little while I would like to go to the store. When do you desire to come?"

Tibbs forced himself to be patient and rational. "How about nine-thirty, would that be all right?"

"I will make some tea," Yumeko volunteered.

Tea again! He didn't especially care for it, but apparently there was no avoiding it. Not where Orientals were concerned, at any rate.

"That will be nice," he said, trying to sound as if he meant it. Then he had another thought. "Yumeko, you remember the two men who came to see you, the policemen you were worried about?"

He sensed her tightening over the wire. He got a hesitant, "Yes."

"After I talk to you, I may ask them to stop by — so that they won't bother you anymore. I will be there to look after you."

"If you say it is good, then it will be all right with me. I am a little frightened of them."

"I think I can end all that."

"Then please to ask them to come. They will drink tea?"

Despite himself Virgil grinned a little with satisfaction. "I'm sure they'd like it very much," he lied cheerfully. "Do you have some nice Japanese green tea?"

"*Ocha?* But yes, I did not know that you liked it. Most Americans, they cannot."

"I'll see you at nine-thirty," Tibbs said and then hung up before things went any farther. Feeling a little better for no real reason that he could trace, he poured some cornflakes into a bowl, covered them with a liberal amount of low-fat milk, and sifted on some sugar. He ate reflectively and planned what he was going to say to the Feds concerning his "discovery," and what they would be likely to say to him if it proved to be a completely wrong assumption. He planned his hedge carefully and then left for his office.

For a wonder the paper work load was not quite as staggering as usual. He disposed of a few things and talked with Agent Jerry Garner, who had been on the stakeout during the graveyard hours. Nothing whatever had happened. That in a way was good news since it suggested if he was right in his assumptions, then he had so far not missed the boat.

When Garner had left he tried a call to the Bureau of Narcotics and Dangerous Drugs and found Duffy in. "I want to put you and Frank in the picture this time," he said. "I had a brainstorm last night which may or may not be good for something, I don't know yet. If it is any good, then I think I can come up with some answers concerning the supply of KB that's been coming in, the connection of Wang with the trade, and where the girl Yumeko Nagashima fits in."

"Do all that and we'll give you a job," Duffy said.

"No thanks, business is good out here most of the time. Understand that all I have so far is a guess, but if it pans out, would you and Frank be free to meet me at the Wang house at a little after ten this morning?"

"Absolutely. Frank's out, but I can raise him."

"Good. Then let me do some checking first; I'll call you if it looks good — or if it doesn't."

"Fair enough, and all kidding aside, Virgil, thank

you very much for the cooperation. This isn't a tea party, you know."

"You could be a little wrong on that, but I understand, and thanks. I'll let you know." He hung up.

As he drove toward the Wang home he rehearsed in his mind exactly how he was going to talk to Yumeko: how much he was going to tell her and how much he was going to withhold. It was not too easy a task and he was parking in front of the house before he was fully settled in his mind as to what he was going to do. As he got out of his car he reluctantly concluded that he would probably have to play things by ear. Normally he did not mind, but Yumeko, being Yumeko, complicated things.

He went up the steps, pushed the doorbell, and waited. In perhaps half a minute the door swung open and he had a mild shock; Yumeko was elaborately dressed in a flowered silk kimono and her hair was piled up in a totally Japanese style. As she bowed low to him, his first reaction was that she must have spent every available minute since his call preparing herself to receive him. As he stood and paused for a moment, uncertain of what he should say, the silence was broken for him. "You like?" she asked.

"Of course, it's beautiful," he answered. Then he found himself a little more. "I wasn't expecting it; you surprised me very much."

She motioned him inside. "It is perhaps not right that I wear kimono because I am only half Japanese. The rest I am what you call here a black girl."

"Negro," Tibbs corrected her. "It's a word to be proud of. You have two heritages instead of just one. And . . ." he paused quite deliberately, ". . . if anyone asks you, you are a very beautiful girl."

She lowered her head. "Because you are yourself Negro and also *shodan*, you are so kind as to say so. Others do not agree."

"Then to hell with them." For a moment he had an urge to kiss her but killed it; it would be all wrong.

"Your friends, they are coming?"

"I think so, but I'm not sure yet. I'd like to ask you a few things first."

"Before tea?"

"Yes — before tea."

With small steps because of her garment, she led the way into the sitting room where they had first met. She sat down on the front of one of the chairs, unable to make herself comfortable because of the elaborate way in which she had tied her obi in the back. She looked at Tibbs as though she were waiting for some sort of judgment to be pronounced.

"Yumeko," he began when he had dropped into a chair, "I have been studying a little about jade and I've learned quite a few things. Am I right in believing that no two jades are alike — that they are all individually created depending on the nature of the raw stone?"

"Yes," she answered. "That is very much true. There are some few things, like incense burners, that are made over and over again almost exactly the same, but these are very ordinary pieces — sometimes not real jade at all."

"But the pieces you would have here in this house would all be individual?"

"That is so. The very common things Mr. Wang would never have."

"All right, so far, so good. Now something else. I'm not asking you to betray any secrets, but where did Mr. Wang get most of his jades? I don't necessarily mean people, I'm talking about places."

Yumeko folded her hands and studied her fingers. "The packages, they came from overseas. From the Far East. Very few from Japan. Mostly they arrived from Singapore, Bangkok, Penang, a few from Hong Kong. There is much jade in Hong Kong, but Mr. Wang would not buy the pieces that came from the communist mainland."

"I see. How about Taiwan — the Republic of China?"

"A few, only a few."

"Any other places?"

"I am not sure; many pieces were here before I came. But there are not many other places where jade is shipped, jade of the best quality."

"So it's a fair conclusion that Singapore, Bangkok, Penang, and perhaps Hong Kong provided more than ninety percent of all the jade that came in to Mr. Wang."

"That is yes."

"Next, did the pieces come one at a time, or did

they come several together in a larger carton or crate?"

"Always they came since I was here each one by itself."

"How often did a piece come in?"

"Not always the same, Virgil. Sometimes for two or three weeks nothing, then several in one week. But always each one alone. Maybe I should say that we received . . . wait — I know the word — average of two each week. Between two and three."

Tibbs shifted his position and recrossed his legs the other way. "Now, Yumeko, when I took that jade to Mr. Harvey, you told me that you were going to put it in *its* box. Then you sorted out several until you found a certain one."

She nodded. "Yes, that is so."

"Now about those blue boxes, they all seem to look alike on the outside, but are they custom-made too? That is, does each jade have its own box especially for it alone?"

"That is yes. The box too is very carefully fitted."

"And the boxes are usually much larger that the jades they hold."

"Yes, there must be room for much padding. Jade is very very hard, but it can also break. That is why the boxes must fit so well."

He got to his feet. "Yumeko, could we go to the jade room and look at some of those boxes?"

She looked at him without understanding. "You wish the boxes?"

"Just to look at them."

With her geta sliding along the floor she led him toward the back of the house and the room where the jade cabinets held their precious contents. She unlocked the door and turned on the lights which brought the multicolored miniature sculptures into a dazzling still life. Still careful to walk around the place where Mr. Wang had lain, she opened the bottom of one of the cabinets and began to remove blue cloth-covered boxes. They varied in size and shape, but otherwise they were monotonously alike. As she handed them up to him, Tibbs put several of them on the table in the center of the room.

Then, while she watched, he began to examine them very carefully. First he lifted each one individually and judged its weight. Then he opened three or four and felt of the padding with the tips of his fingers. All the while Yumeko stood by, watching him but asking no questions. As she watched him, he in turn studied her, but he could detect nothing but an uncertain and rather curious interest in what he was doing.

He picked up each box in turn and carefully inspected the way in which the satin lining had been installed. He studied six of the boxes in this manner and then returned to the one that had been fifth. "Yumeko," he said, "I would like to have your permission to take this box apart a little bit. I'll see to it that it's properly repaired for you."

"Dozo," she answered.

Tibbs took out a penknife, opened the smaller of

the two blades with which it was equipped, and began with careful concentration to loosen the edge of the lining. After a few minutes he had several inches of the satin laid back, exposing an inner muslin covering. He began to work the blade of his knife deeper against the side of the box, being careful to do as little damage as possible. He worked for a good ten minutes before he finally had access to the substantial material that formed the bulk of the stuffing. When he first saw it he gave no signs, but his heart began to beat faster and he knew that it was almost certain that his conjecture had been correct. "May I use your phone?" he asked.

Silently Yumeko inclined her head. Calmly he dialed and waited. When he had Duffy on the line he was very brief. "I'm at the Wang house. I think it would be a good idea if you came over." Then he hung up.

"I do not understand," Yumeko said.

Even though it was still relatively early in the day, Tibbs felt a wave of what might have been fatigue, but he recognized it as relief. "In a few minutes Mr. Lonigan and Mr. Duffy will be coming here," he said. "If you wish to prepare tea for them, now would be the time."

She was not quite sure whether it was a dismissal or not, but she left him. He watched the huge bow of her obi as she retreated toward the kitchen.

When he was alone Tibbs sat down once more and folded his hands in his lap. He pressed his fingers together so tightly they almost seemed to turn white as he thought, evaluating what he had discovered against what he already knew and the few things he still had to learn. There was one awkward little complication that had him stymied and which obstinately refused to yield to logic. He attacked the problem once more, as he had several times before, but the light would not come through the darkness. The thing defied him and he could not crack its defenses.

He leaned back, shut his eyes, and began to go over the whole thing again from the beginning. Once more he fitted the pieces together, as he had done with slips of paper on top of his desk, and filled in the several gaps that he had accumulated enough data to close. But the one damnable thing remained, the one circumstance that he could not explain.

He heard Yumeko busy with her preparations and wondered if things were any easier for her than they were for him. In addition to other immediate problems, she was now effectively alone in a strange country. He had no idea what sort of visa she had, but the fact that she had been admitted into the country at all was unusual in view of the antique and grossly unfair immigration laws which applied to Orientals. The very people who made the best citizens on record were the specific ones who were all but excluded, thanks to legal hangovers of the worst thinking of 1910. Anyway, she *was* in America and at least she had a job. Like most people, she would probably work things out in time.

When the doorbell rang he answered it himself. Lonigan and Duffy were there, and he read on the instant that they had cast themselves in the role of gentlemen callers this time. That made matters a little simpler, because he would not have permitted them to give Yumeko another hard time while he was present. They might be Feds and all that, but he had his own methods and Pasadena was his town.

Yumeko came in and the two narcotics men responded most appropriately to her appearance. They seemed almost relaxed and their manner reflected itself in Yumeko, who began the final preparations for serving with what Tibbs observed to be a decided easing of her former concern. "I believe that we are to have some tea," he said quite formally. "After you've enjoyed that, then I may have some information that might interest you."

"We're fully prepared to be interested," Lonigan said. "You're beginning to live up to your reputation."

"Yes," Duffy contributed. "I hope you had fun playing with those two guys from LAPD."

"We had coffee afterwards," Virgil said.

"Yes, I know. They were almost certain that they had a make on your partner. And it would have been a big one for them."

Tibbs turned serious. "We weren't trying to pick on them, and I had damn good reason for wanting to go on the street. How are things, by the way?"

Lonigan shook his head. "Virgil, the panic is on and

you'd better believe it. The LAPD has half of the drugstores in critical areas staked out, the treatment centers are jammed, and every hour more come in."

"Something else," Duffy added. "We were tipped on another shipment coming up from Mexico. Not a big one this time, but very carefully covered up. Normally it would have gotten through no matter how hard we tried to stop it. We passed the word on to the customs people and they made the grab."

"Is there any heroin in town?"

"I doubt it, Virgil. At least there's not enough for anyone to find. A few junkie dealers may have some stashed away for their own use, but there's none to buy."

"How about keto?"

"There's a little, thank God that's all at the moment. We had two DOA's from it yesterday. Hot-shotted. One was a sixteen-year-old girl: a pretty thing from a good family. Hippie boyfriend, you know the rest."

Yumeko appeared carrying a tray. Lonigan offered to take it from her, but she set it down and began to arrange the tea things. When she was ready she sat down and prepared to play hostess. "I must explain," she said, with her eyes modestly lowered. "Mr. Tibbs, he suggest that I offer you Japanese green tea. This is something which most Americans, I know they do not like. So I make some just for him because he understand it. For you I give the regular black tea — is this all right?" Then she looked up, all innocence.

At that moment Tibbs for the first time seriously wondered if she were really capable of murder. Yumeko was not the simple child that he had unconsciously assumed her to be.

"Excellent," Lonigan said. "I do prefer the black tea and George, Mr. Duffy, does too."

"That is good." Yumeko said. Carefully she poured and served, first the black tea to the federal men, then the thick, bitter green tea to Tibbs and herself. Then, after passing a plate of small cookies, she sat down quietly beside him on the davenport. "I will come here if you allow," she said. "Then you can protect me."

"Touché," Tibbs said.

"I do not understand."

"Mr. Tibbs is admitting that you are a smart girl," Duffy said. "Allow me to second that thought."

"Enjoy your tea, gentlemen," Virgil said. "Then, if you don't mind I'll consult my superiors at our headquarters. After that, I believe I can show you how the drug you have been chasing has been coming into the country." He pulled a small wax evidence envelope out of his coat pocket and handed it to Duffy. "You might check that stuff out," he suggested, indicating a small supply of white crystals that the envelope contained. "If it's what I believe it to be, you have your immediate problem solved."

Duffy's mood changed on the moment. "Virgil, if it is, we can't thank you enough. And you'll get the credit."

Tibbs shook his head. "Skip the credit," he said. "All I want is a murderer."

"Can we help?" Lonigan asked.

"Yes, if you will. Assuming that the lead I'm giving you pans out, I want to ask that you leave things strictly alone and trust our boys for just a short while. Then you can have the whole ball of wax."

"All right, but you understand that we will want to make some arrests."

Tibbs sampled his bitter tea, but refused to let his reaction to it show on his face. "Certainly," he agreed, "but only after I've got my man first."

The doorbell rang. Yumeko rose to answer it, but Tibbs got up too and paused, on his feet, just around the corner. He heard Yumeko say, "Come in," then he waited.

In a moment the visitor came into his line of vision; he was a young man, Chinese or possibly Japanese, and his manner betrayed strong hesitation. Tibbs had seen it too often, the symptoms of suppressed fright or fear. As he stepped out, Yumeko was very quick to perform introductions. "I present you to my friend Mr. Tibbs," she said. "This is Chin Soo, houseboy to Mr. Wang."

Tibbs decided immediately how to play it. "We have been very worried about you," he said. "And Miss Nagashima has been most upset. Are you all right?"

"Yes," the boy said. With the single word he revealed enough English to make communication possible.

"I was about to put out a missing person bulletin on you. Where have you been?"

Chin Soo look sideways as though to assess the possibility of turning and running for his life. Then he accepted the fact that there was no retreat. "I stay away," he said. "I afraid. Man say to go and I go."

"I see. Who was the man who told you to go?"

Chin Soo looked at him, apparently trying to decide whether or not he was compelled to answer that. Once again the avenue of retreat was closed to him, and he had no choice but to reply. "Mr. Johnny Wu," he said.

CHAPTER 13

When Virgil Tibbs walked into his office for the second time that morning there was a note on his desk: *Call Mr. Wu.* He had never received a message that he needed less; at that moment he had a consuming desire to speak with Johnny Wu at the earliest opportunity. He picked up his phone even before he sat down, and dialed.

He got an answer in a slightly singsong feminine voice that very politely told him that Mr. Wu was not in. He was invited to leave his name and number. He did so and hung up, his mind already reaching out to the many other things which he now had to do. He picked up a long pad of yellow ruled paper and began to jot down a series of items that were still unresolved. When he had done that he took off his coat, laid his gun on the desk, and went to work.

He first called the morgue and asked for the surgeon

who had briefed him on the details of Mr. Wang's death. The doctor was in and after something of an interval he came to the telephone. Tibbs asked several questions concerning the damage to the vitality and body structure of the murder victim as a result of the strangling he had received. Presently a little more light began to show. He thanked the assistant coroner for the additional information and made a note on his pad.

He was still writing when the phone rang. He picked it up with the expectation that it would be Johnny Wu, but he was greeted by the voice of Frank Lonigan on the line. "This is very preliminary, Virgil," the federal man told him, "but unless we're completely off the track, that sample that you gave us is the stuff all right. Without a lab report that isn't conclusive, but we expect to have one in a day or two. You've got us pretty excited down here; how can we help you?"

"You just did," Tibbs answered. "For the moment, that's all that I need from your end. I have something planned for tonight that may give us a little more to go on. Would you be available tomorrow?"

"Absolutely. Call this number and they'll reach us — at any hour."

"Outstanding. If anything breaks, you'll hear from me." With that he hung up.

When he had made another note or two he called the LAPD and spoke to the lieutenant who had direct command of the Chinatown detail. From that well-informed officer he gained a number of points concerning which he had been uncertain. Among other things he asked if there had been any recent reports that had indicated new forms of activity in which the police department was interested. When he got a yes answer to that, and such information as the lieutenant had available, he felt like an old fire horse that smells smoke and knows that something in his line is definitely stirring.

His next call was to Lieutenant Olsen's office to find out if there was any report from the stakeout on the Wang home. The reply was almost entirely negative; the houseboy had been seen going to the supermarket and returning with groceries, but the officer who had followed him there had not noted anything amiss.

As soon as he had that information he put in a call to a close friend in Air Force procurement and asked for an informal readout on the Washburn company. He was promised a call back and as much data as could be safely relayed over the telephone. That was all that he required; he followed the call with another note on his pad.

He next phoned the city attorney's office and asked for a background on Aaron Finegold. Fortunately, the man he talked to knew Finegold personally and was able to supply some information that Tibbs was most anxious to have.

After checking the next item on his pad he put in a long-distance call to the narcotics treatment center in

Kentucky and requested a report on Robin Washburn. When he had properly identified himself he was connected with the doctor who had been in charge of the case. He was supplied with the few facts that he required; in addition he learned that the patient had been discharged two days previously and was presumed to have arrived at his home.

Then he remembered something very important that he had all but forgotten. He spun the dial once more and succeeded in getting Yumeko on the line. "I want you to do something for me," he directed. "If anyone calls you on the telephone, anyone at all, I want you to let me know immediately, here at the office. The number is on my card. Do you still have it?"

"I have."

"Good. Be sure to do that — if I'm not here, leave a message for me. I'll get it."

"Do you wish anything else?"

"Yes, I may decide to throw a little party at your home tonight. I would like your permission for that. You might have to serve some more tea and some biscuits, but I'll pay the cost."

"There will be no cost. I can."

"Excellent. And, Yumeko, don't worry — you'll be fully protected."

"I have not worry."

"I'll probably stop in to see you this afternoon," he concluded, and then hung up. His mind was all business now, and he knew at least one thing about

Yumeko that made him keep his guard up. Like so many others in this peculiar case, she had not been entirely candid with him. People seldom were when murder was involved.

His phone rang. He picked it up once more and was gratified to hear Johnny Wu at the other end of the line. "I want to talk to you very much," Tibbs said, "and as soon as possible."

"That's fine with me, Virgil," Wu replied. "As a matter of fact I'm coming out to Pasadena — I want to see Yumeko Nagashima. Do you have any objection to that?"

It was a loaded question. "Of course not, why shouldn't you call on her if you want to. Is she expecting you?"

"I called her a few minutes ago."

Tibbs was furious with himself; he had carefully asked the girl to report all future calls, but he had failed to ask her about any that might have come in since he had left her. "What time is your appointment, Johnny?" he asked.

"I left it open, but I was planning to offer her lunch if she would like."

Virgil glanced at his watch. "Since there's time, would you mind stopping by here on your way? We're not hard to find."

"I'll be glad to. Say in half an hour?"

"Good. See you then."

As he hung up the instrument, Bob Nakamura came in. In contrast to his usual brisk manner he seemed thoroughly exhausted. He dropped into his chair and then carefully rubbed his face with his hands. "What news?" Virgil asked.

"They're bagged; the Feds nabbed them when they were trying to board a plane at Hollywood-Burbank. One of them made a dive for it, but all he did was bust himself up."

"Evidence?"

"With what I've been able to get, and the others, there's enough to put them inside about six times over. They turned out to be wanted in a half a dozen other places. It's a federal rap now, so they'll be out of the way for quite a while."

"Congratulations," Tibbs said. "You must have been on that one for almost two months."

"Actually a little more than that."

"Then why don't you take the afternoon off? Then you'll be fresh to go to work with me this evening."

Bob turned a look at him that would have made a stone weep. "What is it now, Virg, out on the street again?"

Tibbs shook his head. "On the contrary, I'd like you to be my guest at a little party. I don't believe that you've met any of the principals in my case, have you?"

"Give me a list, but I don't think so."

"I will. Tonight, if all goes well, you will be Mr. Nakamura, the representative of a group of wealthy Oriental art dealers."

Bob raised a warning hand. "Hold it, Virg. I can

speak Japanese, but if that girl you told me about is going to be there, she'll spot my American accent the first time I open my mouth. I'll never get away with it."

"You don't have to; I may just create the impression that you are from Hawaii. You are present because you are interested in acquiring the jade collection of the late, respected dealer whom you knew only by reputation."

"I see. Am I an eager beaver, or what?"

"You are an efficient, very capable, reasonably polite businessman. You have substantial financial resources behind you."

"Would that it were true."

"Shut up — you have me for a friend, don't you? It will be at the Wang place this evening, say around nine. Wear your good suit."

"One question," Bob interjected. "Am I representing Japanese or American interests?"

Tibbs thought a moment. "That's a good point. Imply that they're Japanese, but avoid a flat statement."

"And if I get blown?"

"Then leave everything to me. Of those who I expect will be present you can trust me — nobody else, got that?"

"It sounds like a charming affair. At least it's different. I'll come by a few minutes after nine. Who invited me?"

"I did — we're acquainted. Leave it at that."

That matter settled, Tibbs turned to the inevitable accumulation of paper work and began to hoe his way through. He was still at it when the reception desk in the lobby called to inform him that Johnny Wu had arrived. "Send him up in two minutes," he said, allowing enough time for Bob Nakamura to make his disappearance. When Johnny's well-rounded bulk appeared in the doorway, Tibbs was alone.

He motioned his guest to a chair, and then lost no time in coming to the point. "Johnny," he began, "I don't think that you've been leveling with me. Chin Soo showed up this morning at the Wang house. I happened to be there. He told me that you had advised him to make himself scarce just at a time when I was very anxious to talk to him."

"All right," Johnny admitted, "I was dead wrong on that and all I can do at this point is to offer you an apology — and an explanation."

"Skip the apology, but I'm very interested in the explanation."

Johnny rested an arm on Tibbs' desk. "Within the Chinese-American community we like to handle our own problems. We seldom appeal to the police for help, and we don't usually ask for charity. We take care of our own."

"I know that."

"Good. Chin Soo is, of course, Chinese. Virgil, can I talk off the record for a little bit?"

"Provisionally, yes."

"Make it definitely; there's a good reason. Take my word for it."

"All right."

"Off the record, then, Chin Soo is in this country legally, but just barely. If the full facts were to be published, he might face deportation. And that would be very undesirable; he's a sound young man and a very honest one."

Virgil nodded, but said nothing.

"When Wang Fu-sen was killed, Chin panicked, and I can't honestly blame him. He had never established a rapport with Miss Nagashima and for family reasons, he distrusts all Japanese. Now you know that Fu-sen and I were friends; it was at his house that I met Chin — not socially in that sense of the word, but we were introduced. So when he discovered what had happened to his employer, he had immediate visions of being interviewed by the police and having his status come out. That would mean back to Hong Kong and for very good and honorable reasons, he didn't want any of that. So he took an immediate powder and came to see me."

Johnny leaned forward to give emphasis to what he was about to say. "Now I give you my word that if you had shown any interest in the houseboy, or had asked me about him, I would have told you what I knew. But when you didn't bring it up I kept my mouth shut and you can't honestly blame me too much for that."

"Go on," Tibbs said.

"I can tell you this: Chin doesn't know a damn things about Fu-sen's death that you haven't already been told, I determined that to my own satisfaction. If I had felt that he had any real information or evidence to give you, I would have made him come forward. Enough of that. When things began to take a different turn, I made a decision to send him back to the house. In the first place it was his responsibility — the death of Fu-sen didn't relieve him of his obligations. He owed Wang a great deal and it was up to him to pay off. He had two things to do: to continue to take care of the house for the time being and to protect the Nagashima girl, because Fu-sen had been interested in her — as an object of his generosity."

Tibbs picked up a pencil and rubbed it between his palms. "How much 'protection' do you think he might be able to provide? And why do you think that Yumeko might need it?"

Johnny Wu smiled at that. "Virgil, have you ever heard of *Gung Fu*?"

"Yes — Chinese karate — or the equivalent."

"Roughly that's right, except I personally think that you're underrating it a little. Anyhow, Chin happens to be an expert; accept my assurance that he's mighty damn good."

"All right, I'll buy that," Tibbs said. "But why the sudden need for protection?"

This time Johnny pulled out his handkerchief and

used it to wipe his hands. "This is the part that you will want to know," he said. "And I admit that I should have told you sooner. I was following tradition instead of common sense and you have my apology. The fact that Chin Soo was in Wang Fu-sen's house was not entirely an accident. Some time ago some of us in our community became aware of the fact that Wang was being put under some kind of unpleasant pressure. The details weren't available and no one was about to ask him, that would have been outside of our rules of conduct, but we had a pretty good idea. The Chicoms try to make it hot for us every now and then if they think that there is anything to be gained by it. If you care to check with the FBI, they may tell you that I value my citizenship and have done a few things to earn it."

"By the Chicoms, you mean the Chinese communists."

"Right. To them we are overseas Chinese and they mean to use us in any way that they can. When the word came through that Fu-sen was having some difficulties, we looked for a good man. Chin Soo was recommended and he wanted desperately to come to America — as practically all of our better displaced young people do. We sent for him and after his arrival he did his stuff for a *Gung Fu* master who approved his ability. Then we put him into Wang's home — with appropriate courtesy, of course. Fu-sen understood. We wanted the bodyguard to have a gun also, but Wang absolutely balked at that: he abhorred violence of any kind. About three months after that the Nagashima girl arrived from Japan. I can guess your next thought, but forget it. Chin has undergone severe training and intense discipline — so despite natural inclinations he wouldn't overstep in the house of his employer and, as I said, he doesn't dig Japanese."

"A blind spot," Virgil said.

"Granted. Now you asked me why we thought that protection might be necessary for the girl — as of now. I was about to tell you this anyway, but I hasten to add that I just learned of it myself. There is some new strong-arm talent in town."

Tibbs leaned forward. "Chinese?" he asked.

Wu nodded. "Yes — or possibly Korean; I can't be certain because I haven't seen them. But the word gets around. There are two of them and the reports are that they are tough — very tough."

"How did they get into this country?"

"Virgil, forgive me, but don't be naïve. How many Mexicans do you imagine there are living here right now who never entered through formal channels? We have largely open borders and if someone wants to get in and has the resources, he can make it. Orientals don't try it too much because we're conspicuous and suspected, but it goes on every day. It isn't advertised, because it would only encourage the traffic. It's pretty tough to tell an honest, hardworking Chinese who would like to immigrate here that the present U.S.

laws give him almost no chance whatever because he isn't a Caucasian. It's a medieval relic, Virgil, and it forces otherwise honest people to step around the law sometimes, as we frankly did to bring in Chin Soo."

"Have you anything else you can tell me about the imported talent?"

"Yes. It won't stand up in court as evidence, but we know. The two hard types are either Chicoms or possibly North Koreans who are passing as something else. That's easy here because so few of the majority can tell the difference. And we have good reason to think that they're in the narcotics business."

Virgil shook his head. "Johnny, I can't keep that to myself: assuming that you're right, it's too important. I'll protect the rest of your information as much as I can, but that is something I've got to pass on."

"All right, I understand. Just forget where you heard it, that's all. I'm a peaceful man."

"Something else," Tibbs continued. "I understand that there is to be a meeting this evening, at the Wang home, to discuss the possible disposal of the jade collection presently housed there."

Wu suddenly sat up straighter in his chair. "Could I arrange to be in on that?" he asked.

Tibbs was calm. "I'm sure there's no problem. It's to be at nine, I'm told that some of the other guests can't make it before then."

"Nine it is. Anything else?"

"Yes, as a matter of fact. I'd like word of the meeting to filter through to the two visitors you just told me about. Can you handle it?"

"You mean to invite them?"

"No, just to let them know."

"May I use your phone?"

Tibbs pushed it over. Johnny picked it up and dialed; when he had his number he began a rapid-fire conversation in Chinese. He was on the line for some time, long enough to make Virgil wonder what was actually being said. The Negro detective waited patiently until Johnny was through and then looked at his guest for a report.

"One thing about our community," Johnny said, "we have good communications. They'll hear."

"Do you know where to find them?" Virgil asked.

"No, but by the middle of the afternoon they should have the word, wherever they are. Anything else?"

"That's it until tonight."

Without ceremony, Johnny left.

As soon as he was alone Tibbs put in one more call, this one long-distance to Gumps, the famous jade store in San Francisco. His two or three questions were promptly and courteously answered by someone who was clearly an expert. He already knew the essential facts he was given, but they served to confirm a guess that he had made and which, in the light of the new evidence, looked better and better to him. In this improved frame of mind he went to lunch.

By the time he returned, there was a message for

him from the LAPD which confirmed another of his ideas. He began a fresh series of phone calls. The first was to Aaron Finegold. He invited him to be present that evening in order to protect the interests of his client, Miss Yumeko Nagashima. On that premise Finegold consented to come. He also agreed to see Tibbs for a few minutes later that afternoon.

Don Washburn agreed to shift an evening appointment to comply with Virgil's request to come to the Wang home.

Harvey, the stock trader, was cool when he answered the phone, but warmed somewhat when he heard his caller's name. "I'm glad you're in touch, Mr. Tibbs," he said. "I'd like to express my regret for my shortness with you when you came to my home. The news is out now that my wife and I are separating. We had had a particularly painful disagreement at some length just before you came to see me. I fear that I was not at my best."

That provided Virgil with an opening and he used it. When he hung up less than a minute later, he had Harvey's assurance that he would be at the meeting.

If anything plagued him, it was the fact that at many points in the case he was building he lacked the vital element of proof. No conclusions he reached meant a thing until he could support them with solid evidence in court. That he would still have to obtain. And he was not so optimistic as to assume that if he confronted the guilty person or persons, he would be immediately rewarded with full confessions given in the presence of reliable witnesses. As was practically always the case, he would have to do it the hard way.

He began by going to see Aaron Finegold. He could have saved himself the errand with a phone call, but he had his own reasons for appearing in person. He was admitted after a short wait; the attorney shook hands and then waved him to a chair. That done he sat down himself and waited for Tibbs to begin.

Virgil obliged. "Unless there is some very strong reason why you can't do so, I'd appreciate it very much if you would announce this evening that the jade collection that was Mr. Wang's is going to Miss Naga-shima."

Finegold pondered. "It might be rushing things a bit," he said.

"Possibly so, but I have an excellent reason for asking this."

"One connected with the administration of justice?"

"Yes."

"Then I'll have to go along, I guess. My wife is very impressed with you, by the way."

"In the police business we can use all of the appreciation that we can get," Tibbs responded. "And if I may, the feeling is entirely mutual."

"She'll be happy to hear that."

From the lawyer's office he drove directly to the

Wang home. Chin Soo opened the door and smiled when he saw Tibbs' dark face. "We glad you come."

Virgil caught something in the tone of his voice. After he was inside and the door was shut, he turned again to the houseboy. "How much English do you really speak?" he asked.

Soo hesitated a moment, then replied. "More than I admit."

"I thought so. Where did you learn it?"

"In Hong Kong. It's a British colony, you know."

"But more than ninety-eight percent Chinese."

"True, but I got around."

"Officially?"

Chin shook his head. "Nothing like that. But I have some friends."

"Have any of them come calling here lately?"

Soo looked at him more intently for a moment. "I see you have the word. They're on the other side as far as I'm concerned."

"A couple of things," Tibbs said. "First, if anything breaks tonight, let me handle it. Don't attempt anything on your own."

Soo inclined his head slightly. "Excuse me, but you are not Chinese. If those two come, it will be my problem."

"Do you carry a concealed weapon?"

"I am the weapon, Mr. Tibbs."

"Not against two armed men, you aren't."

"For either of them to fire a gun, he would have to take it out first. That takes time."

For the moment Virgil did not elect to pursue the matter. "Do you have access to the jade room?" he asked.

"Mr. Wang gave me full responsibility for its care."

"Good. And I appreciate the protection you gave him, even though you were not able to prevent what occurred."

"He dispatched me on a long errand, Mr. Tibbs, me and the girl. Quite obviously he wanted us out of the way. Most reluctantly I obeyed him. I do not like to leave this house unguarded."

"Even now?"

"Yes, even now. I was assigned here for that purpose."

"Can you prove that?"

"Mr. Wu could perhaps help you."

"Is it the jades?"

Chin Soo shook his head. "It is something else."

"Some people have named it 'jade dust.' "

Chin bowed. "You are most intelligent; you should be Chinese. You know also, then, that Mr. Wang was a most honorable man."

"I know."

"There is evil in this house, Mr. Tibbs. It will shortly be taken away and disposed of by reliable people. Until that occurs, it is my responsibility to keep it here."

"I'm for that," Virgil said, "and because I am, I want you to do something for me. How many boxes do you suspect contain the forbidden drug?"

"Perhaps one half."

"In weight?"

"As much as four hundred pounds."

"As a heroin substitute on the street, then, it could be worth as much as six million dollars."

"More, much more. And it is not a substitute, Mr. Tibbs, it is a replacement. A replacement that would be almost entirely controlled from one source."

"Here is what I want you to do," Tibbs said. "Find several boxes of different sizes that do not contain the drug — can you do that?"

"Of course."

"Since the boxes all look the same from the outside, is it true that the only way to identify them is by the individual jade each is built to contain?"

"That is correct."

"If for any reason a jade goes out of this house, you will put it into its box."

Chin Soo bowed again. "I understand. There will be no problem; such a mistake will be easy to make."

"Good. Where is Yumeko, by the way?"

"She is resting, preparing herself for this evening."

"One more thing: how well do you know the value of the pieces in the collection?"

"I know the value and also the price that Mr. Wang would have asked."

"Then that takes care of everything. I will be back before seven tonight; I suggest that you eat very early."

"Excuse me, Mr. Tibbs, but we were expecting that you would join us."

Virgil shook his head. "I still have some things to do. Watch yourself in the meantime."

Chin Soo led him back to the door. "Do not concern yourself about that," he said as he ushered Tibbs out.

During the short drive back to headquarters the police radio chattered with minor dispatches. An abandoned car was checked out for the name of the owner. A citizen assist call for a police officer turned out to be a request for help in moving a heavy refrigerator. A suspicious person reported lurking in the vicinity of an apartment building was found to be a completely legitimate florist's deliveryman. And so it went, the endless parade of details in the life and operation of a modern city. People called the police for everything — once for a suitable escort to take a roommate to a party. Anything and everything came over the police radio. Floyd Sanderson had been on patrol one night when he had been dispatched to investigate "a male Oriental eating the grass." He had arrived to find the call quite genuine, a male Oriental *was* eating the grass. Like the members of every community represented in the city, a few Orientals had mental disturbances and this had been one of them. Sanderson had helped the man, turned him over to the proper medical authorities, and then had gone back on patrol. A hundred or more miles every night, cruising endlessly up and down the streets, in order to meet and deal with whatever unusual circumstances might arise — from a drunk asleep on the sidewalk to a fleeing murderer armed and volcanically dangerous.

For what he hoped would be the last time that day Tibbs walked into his office and found Bob there. "All set for tonight?" the Nisei detective asked.

Virgil sat for a moment on the edge of his desk. "It looks good. One thing I want you to do: not too soon, but when things are well along, I want you to ask if you can come back tomorrow night to examine the jade collection. Remember that you have not yet seen it, you know of it only by reputation. A casual look around won't do — you want to make a detailed study."

"Sounds logical."

"I hope so. Don't overplay it; there'll be some bright people there."

"I won't. Lieutenant Olsen wants to know if you still need the stakeout at the Wang house."

"Hell yes, I'm depending on it."

"OK, I'll pass the word. Next: are we likely to be bringing in a prisoner tonight?"

"I doubt it."

"Since you're getting everyone together, I thought you were going to spring your case."

"Not yet. I know what I'm after, but I don't have the proof — and that's the most vital part."

"What's the plan?"

Once more Tibbs took off his coat before he sat down. "I'm going to try and do it an easier way," he said. "This whole deal is set up for one reason — to make the guilty person panic a little. If I can pull that off and force one more piece of action, then I've got it."

"What kind of action?"

"You'll know," Virgil promised.

CHAPTER 14

At a few minutes before seven Virgil Tibbs parked his car a little more than a block away from the Wang home, locked it, and then continued on foot. As he walked up the quiet street there was no visible indication of the stakeout which was still in operation; at least none which an unsuspecting layman would be likely to notice. He had already passed certain instructions to Agent Jerry Garner, who was heading the crew, and knew that they would be followed explicitly. With his preparations as close to complete as he could make them, he turned in at the driveway, mounted the steps, and rang the front doorbell.

Chin Soo admitted him almost at once. The young Chinese houseboy was dressed in dark slacks and a lightweight black sweater which emphasized the lean strength of his body. Tibbs glanced at his feet and noted the slip-on shoes which, if necessary, could be shed within a second or two. He was not familiar with the techniques of *Gung Fu*, but the years of rigorous training which he himself had undergone had taught him a great deal — including the fact that the bare feet of a karate man are among his most lethal weapons. Chin Soo's costume, he judged, had been chosen for action, even though it did not loudly proclaim that fact.

"Good evening, sir," Chin said. "I am very glad that you have arrived."

"Thank you."

"The jade boxes have been arranged as you asked," he continued. "I have not had time to determine which of the others . . ."

He stopped when Yumeko appeared, very simply dressed in blouse and skirt. "Good evening, Virgil," she said. "I have not yet made myself ready because first I ask you what you wish I wear."

"That's up to you," Tibbs answered. "It's not a party, if that's what you mean." He turned to face her squarely. "I want you to do something: stay out of this part of the house. And keep out of sight. If the doorbell rings, don't come, we'll answer it."

She looked at him very steadily. "You are expecting people to come with trouble."

"Possibly," he admitted, "but nothing we can't handle." He looked at her, as he had several times before, accustoming himself to the combination of Japanese features and Negro complexion. He was not disturbed by it, but he found himself thinking of her as entirely a Japanese, then in the next moment as a Negro girl who had grown up in a foreign country. There was a delicacy to her features that was definitely Oriental, and her eyes, of course, had smooth upper lids. But she was dark enough to pass almost anywhere as a Negro; only her face really betrayed the fact that she had had any other origin.

If the Japanese won out in his mind, it was because of her name and the fact that to her, English was a difficult foreign language. If she had been called Nancy or something like that, and had spoken with the same fluency that he did, it could easily have gone the other way.

"Now," he said, "it may be that someone tonight will want to come and see you tomorrow evening; in fact I'll try to arrange that. Yumeko, I want you to say that you are very sorry, but that you will not be at home; you and Chin Soo are going into Los Angeles to the Buddhist temple to keep a prayer vigil for Mr. Wang."

"There are Buddhist temples here," Soo said.

"Don't bring that up. There are different kinds of temples, I know that; they will assume that you want to visit a certain one. It doesn't matter whether you're Buddhist or not, they'll believe you."

"Mr. Wang was," Chin said, "so it is very logical that we would go to his church to pray for him."

"That's fine. Let the assumption be that you will be

there for some time. And please be sure to convey the idea that you are going together — that's important."

"It shall be so," Yumeko said.

"I have read of things like this," Chin interjected. "Are you going to gather everyone together tonight and then announce who killed Mr. Wang?"

"It isn't that simple."

"Not like Mr. Nero Wolfe."

"I'm afraid not. Not being a genius, I have to do things the difficult way."

"I think that you will succeed."

"Thank you. Now let's get down to business. Yumeko, you get dressed in whatever way you like, but keep it informal — no kimono this time. Then let Chin and me handle things until we send for you."

"I will wish to make preparations in the kitchen."

"That's all right, but keep the doors closed and don't come out here."

She looked at him with dark eyes. "You will not allow me because I am female," she said.

"I don't want you to get hurt — just in case," Tibbs answered. Then he took her by the shoulders and turned her around. "Be good," he admonished.

When she had gone Chin spoke. "It is good that you send her away. We will now await the arrival of the two Chinese who were here before."

"Are you expecting them?" Virgil asked.

"No, sir, but I believe that you are."

"Possibly — I can't be sure." With that he walked

into the living room, chose a place where he could keep a careful watch on the door, and sat down. From the side pocket of his coat he drew out a pocketbook-sized copy of Kawabata's *Snow Country* and began quietly to read.

After a few minutes Chin Soo set down a cup of hot coffee at his elbow. Otherwise it was quiet in the house; the houseboy's shoes had soft soles which were silent on the carpeting, few street noises filtered through the heavy draperies which hung closed before the windows. Yumeko had effectively disappeared. With the calm patience that he had developed during the past several years of police work Tibbs read on, his mind fully absorbed by the text before him while he waited.

Presently he began to feel a little tired; the strains of the past several days asserted themselves, inviting him to close his eyes. In response he stirred himself and reached for the coffee cup, but it was already empty. A glance at his watch told him that it was ten minutes after eight.

He stood up, stretched, and then once more settled down with his book. He read steadily after that until the doorbell finally rang at eight minutes to nine.

Chin Soo materialized to answer it and admitted Johnny Wu. With a properly smiling face the Chinese-American entrepreneur came in, his hand outstretched to greet Tibbs. "I'm glad to see you," he said. "I was afraid I was the first."

In the background Chin looked a question at Tibbs and read the very slight, all but invisible nod that he received in return. By the time Johnny had settled himself and was fumbling for a pack of cigarettes, Yumeko came into the room. In accordance with Tibbs' suggestion she had put on a quite simple, but very tasteful dress that set her off to excellent advantage. As though to emphasize the Japanese side of her background, she had arranged her long hair in a completely Oriental style, piled up on her head in a manner which suggested an Utamaro print. It was altogether captivating and Virgil was fully aware of it.

A second ring of the doorbell announced Elliot Harvey, the stock trader. As he walked into the room Virgil noted a visible change in his manner; his temperament was still austere, but he was clearly prepared to make an effort to be congenial. He shook hands with Tibbs and with Johnny Wu, then turned to greet Yumeko almost as an afterthought. As he did so, and perhaps took clear notice of her for the first time, he reacted enough for Virgil to take note of the fact. He appeared to acknowledge her advantages and if he felt any hesitation toward her because of her origins, he gave no indication of that whatsoever.

Within the next five minutes Aaron Finegold arrived with his wife. Immediately behind them came Donald Washburn who, somewhat surprisingly, had brought his son with him. As Tibbs shook hands with the lad he observed his thin torso and other external evidence of inadequate physical development. Since his father was conspicuously virile, the contrast was acute, but Washburn showed every indication of being proud of his boy.

Although the living room was not notably large, Yumeko made her guests comfortable with an easy manner which belied her fear of social contacts. Chin Soo provided additional chairs as they were required, placing them in locations which he had apparently selected well beforehand.

The last to appear of the invited guests was Bob Nakamura. His protective coloration was complete; his amiable round face did not suggest the imbecile, nor did the well-tailored suit that he wore, but there was nothing whatever about him which fitted the image of a police officer. He looked precisely like an Oriental-American businessman, and by his demeanor he carried off the role to perfection.

When the company had settled down, Virgil casually opened the meeting. "Thank you all for coming here tonight," he began. "I appreciate it very much." He paused a moment and looked about the room. "You know whose house this was and something of the circumstances of his passing. They are under investigation at the present time, and that is my excuse for being here myself this evening."

He paused once more, but everyone was quite content to let him continue. In a corner of the room closest to the front door Chin Soo stood so quietly that he was half invisible. Yumeko was tense despite her outward composure — he knew her well enough now to read that. In some respects, he was aware, she had reason to be.

"There are at least two people not present here this evening whom I'm very much interested in interviewing concerning Mr. Wang's death," Tibbs continued. "When I will be able to do that is uncertain. In the meantime some other matters should be attended to. Mr. Finegold, would you care to explain to us the present and future status of Mr. Wang's very beautiful and valuable jade collection?"

The lawyer easily took the floor without moving from his chair. As he spoke, Virgil carefully watched the developing interest in his words. He sat very still, appearing to give Finegold his attention, but he was acutely aware of the human reactions about him and he weighed them against the conclusions that he had in his mind. It took Finegold more than four minutes to lay his groundwork, then, without histrionics, he made the announcement that according to the provisions which Mr. Wang had made, the jade collection in its entirety had been left to Miss Yumeko Nagashima. A second or two later the girl herself seemed to have been suddenly stricken; her hands flew up and covered her face. Then, shortly, her body began to shake with suppressed sobs.

There was no one in the room who was not looking at her, understanding that she had had no intimation that she was to receive so magnificent a bequest — or any at all. Tibbs watched her too, then he observed the others, including Chin Soo. The houseboy was also looking at Yumeko, but his features told less than those of anyone else present.

Presently the girl recovered somewhat and reached for her handkerchief. Decently, the others gave her an opportunity to recover herself. She wiped her eyes several times and then looked at Finegold with bewilderment. "Are you sure?" she asked.

The attorney nodded. "I drew up the will. It was Mr. Wang's clear and unequivocal wish. So the collection is now yours. You understand, however, that there will be an inheritance tax and that the estate will have to go through probate before it will be free and clear. I'll be glad to handle that for you if you so desire."

At that point Tibbs interjected a question. "Mr. Finegold, in view of the high value of the collection, and the fact that Miss Nagashima was totally unprepared for the announcement that she is an heiress, do you consider it possible that you might get court permission for her to sell a few pieces in order to raise the necessary costs?"

"That's entirely possible, providing we can get a reliable appraisal from a qualified expert of the pieces she might wish to sell."

"I would suggest Mr. Wu," Virgil said. "He is himself a jade dealer and should easily qualify as an expert."

Bob Nakamura entered the conversation. "Mr. Finegold, I represent certain highly reliable people who have considerable resources behind them. Not unlimited, of course, but substantial. On Mr. Tibbs' recommendation I will be glad to accept Mr. Wu as an expert on jade and its value, both wholesale and retail. I also have some slight knowledge of the subject. With Miss Nagashima's permission, I should like to examine the collection with a view to making a flat offer for it *in toto*. If the offer is acceptable, then we would assume the responsibility for advancing the necessary funds to clear it through probate."

Harvey, the stock trader, was next. "Mr. Finegold, I take it that you are representing Miss Nagashima this evening?"

"At present I am her attorney of record, yes. That is in response to a request made by Mr. Wang."

"Understood. My business is investments, sir, and I too know something about jade." He turned toward Bob. "I'm sorry that I didn't get your name."

"Nakamura."

"Mr. Nakamura, it was my intention since shortly after I learned of Mr. Wang's death to make an offer, when the time was proper, for the collection. As a matter of business, as I am sure it is with you."

"I have taken note of that, sir," Finegold answered, "and subject to Miss Nagashima's instructions I will be more than happy to give you an opportunity to bid."

"I too would like to examine the collection."

"I, personally, see no objection to that."

"Thank you." Harvey looked around the room. "Anyone else?"

Don Washburn responded. "I am frankly not in a position to make an offer for the entire collection, largely because I am not in the business in any way and would have no machinery to make subsequent sales. I'm a collector, pure and simple. But if I may, I would like to have the opportunity to acquire three or four pieces that I have had under consideration. If it works out that Miss Nagashima does wish to make some sales to pay probate and estate costs, then I will be a willing customer. And I'll be glad to accept Mr. Wu's evaluation as to what would be a fair and proper price."

"I'm in somewhat the same position myself," Finegold said, and looked toward his wife. "We too have had our eye, so to speak, on certain pieces which we have neglected to acquire largely because I have been heavily engaged in court for some weeks. As a matter of fact I had asked Mr. Wang to give us first refusal on them in case anyone else expressed interest in the interim."

"I'm sure that my principals would respect that commitment," Bob Nakamura said. He removed his glasses and wiped them so convincingly that Virgil was almost persuaded himself that his business negotiations were entirely bona fide.

"This is not properly my affair in any way," Tibbs

said quietly, "but I would like to make a suggestion if I may. If Miss Nagashima feels up to it, perhaps she would consent to open the jade room. Then Mr. and Mrs. Finegold can indicate the pieces in which they are interested. After that Mr. Washburn can do the same. If there is no conflict, then their priority will be established. If there is a conflict, then they can resolve it by mutual consultation."

Harvey apparently had been thinking. "If it is agreeable with everyone," he declared, "I would like to have the same privilege. I too am a collector and if I do not acquire the entire collection, there are some pieces I would like to buy individually."

Finegold took the floor once more. "It strikes me that Mr. Tibbs' suggestion is a very fair and equitable one." He turned to Yumeko. "Miss Nagashima, how do you feel?"

The girl swallowed before she answered. "It is, I think, most right to do this, but I ask to be excused. I wish to serve tea. I ask that you allow Mr. Chin Soo to showing the jades." She turned and looked at the houseboy, who bowed.

"I am happy," he said.

"I don't see any point in who goes first," Washburn said. "I suggest that Mr. and Mrs. Finegold go, then Mr. Harvey, and I'll be glad to bring up the rear."

Harvey nodded his acceptance of that. As the Finegolds got up, Yumeko quietly slipped out of the room; she had still not recovered from the surprise announcement and appeared to be in an aura of disbelief.

Virgil looked at Finegold. "May I come with you?" he asked.

"Please."

By Tibbs' watch it took the Finegolds exactly eight minutes from the moment they entered the jade room until they had indicated four choices to the houseboy, who had made careful notes on a piece of paper.

Harvey required nine minutes and twenty-three seconds to choose three items.

Don Washburn spent some three and a half minutes showing his son the general wonder of the jade room, then he took precisely three minutes and fifty-four seconds to point out three items to Chin Soo. "I've seen them all before," he explained.

When he had returned to the living room with his son, Tibbs looked a question at Chin Soo who shook his head in reply. Of the ten jades chosen, none was duplicated. "You know what to do now, don't you?" Virgil said.

"I understood as soon as you made the suggestion, Mr. Tibbs. Are you sure that you don't have a little Chinese blood somewhere in your ancestry?"

"I'm afraid not. As far as I know my background is pure Negro; none of my female forebears appears to have been raped by white slave owners."

"Then you are probably an exception," Chin said. "But if there is a fountain of intelligence, your ancestors drank from it. I did not kill my employer, sir, but if I had, I would have good reason to be fearful now."

Virgil turned. "Let's go back," he suggested. "Yumeko may need moral support." He waited while the jade room was carefully secured, then he followed the houseboy back to the living room where Yumeko was in the act of serving. As Tibbs sat down she handed him a cup, he glanced inside and saw that this time the tea was black. "Thank you," he said.

She lowered her eyes. "It is my poor best. Please forgive me."

Bob Nakamura spoke to her from a short distance away, but his words could be generally heard in the room. "I don't want to inconvenience you this evening, but I would appreciate it if I could call on you tomorrow evening and have the privilege of seeing your jades. So far I know them only by reputation."

She turned to face him. "It would make me the greatest pleasure, Nakamura san, but tomorrow evening I am going with Chin Soo to temple. It is to make prayer vigil for Mr. Wang. It is much in my heart that I go there."

Tibbs was impressed by the quality of her performance; she had spoken in such a quiet, yet sincere manner that she had been totally convincing. He almost believed her himself. Once again he noted that there were depths to Yumeko that were far from being visible on the surface.

He caught the eye of Aaron Finegold and gave him a

very slight nod. The attorney picked it up and in a few moments spoke generally. "Since Mr. Wang assigned me the responsibility for handling his estate as well as other matters, I'd like to thank you all very much for coming here this evening. I believe that we have a fully mutual understanding. Are there any questions that any of you would like to ask?"

Don Washburn responded. "I'd like to ask Mr. Tibbs if he has any announcements that he was planning to make."

Virgil shook his head. "Not at this time."

"I understand, but naturally I'm anxious. I'm sure that we all are."

There was a general stir of leaving. Harvey went first, followed by the Washburns, but Johnny Wu lingered. As soon as Bob Nakamura was well out of the door, he spoke to Finegold. "I didn't have a good opportunity to bring this up before," he said, "but I am also very much interested in the jade stock. Mr. Tibbs can tell you that I'm an established dealer and I invite you to check my credit standing." He looked about him, making sure who was present and who was not. "I don't believe that the others quite realize this, but if the stock is about as I last saw it, the value should be in the vicinity of half a million dollars."

Yumeko gasped.

"That's a pretty substantial investment," Johnny continued. "I'm prepared to make two proposals for you and Miss Nagashima to consider. First, I will undertake to sell whatever amount of the collection you would like at a reasonable rate of commission. Some of the pieces are individually quite exceptional: there are some lavender ones that command a very high premium. I will guarantee to protect your client's interests by seeing that they are not sold below their value in the current market. Or, if you would prefer, I will purchase pieces outright up to a reasonable quantity and at equitable prices — you can depend on me for that."

Finegold nodded his head. "That sounds very fair both ways, Mr. Wu. Let's leave it at this for tonight: I'll keep your offer very clearly in mind and give you a full opportunity in any competitive situation if one develops. Your being an established dealer is a strong point in your favor."

"Thank you. May I also remind you that I was Wang Fu-sen's close friend; by our standards that leaves me with a very definite obligation under the present circumstances."

"I appreciate that. Thank you, Mr. Wu."

When the last of the guests had left, Virgil turned to Yumeko and Chin. "Both of you did very well this evening," he said. "I'm sorry that I had to put you to so much trouble, but there was a good reason for it."

"I am aware," Chin Soo answered. "What are we to do tomorrow?"

"I'll call you. I recommend that you stay here until

I do." He was too mentally tired to suggest anything else. He had been on very keen edge all evening and it was telling on him.

"A cup of coffee before you go?" Chin asked.

"No, thanks. I want to go home and go to bed. Thank you both again." With that he left and walked back to his car.

It took him less than fifteen minutes to drive home and park. Then he went up to his apartment and phoned the night-watch commander, Lieutenant Olsen. "I may have stirred something up tonight," he reported. "If I was successful, then something should break soon — possibly later tonight, but tomorrow evening looks like a much better bet. After that it should be all over. Can you keep the stakeout going?"

"Of course, Virgil. If you need more help, let me know."

"Right now everything looks fine. If anything does let go tonight, call me here right away, please. Otherwise, good night."

He was ready then for a drink. He mixed himself one and sat down to enjoy it, trying to think of something besides the case and all of its ramifications. It was a weird one and he was perhaps the only one who knew how really weird it was in all of its aspects.

The jade book on the table beside him invited attention. He picked it up, opened to where he had stopped his last period of study, and began to read. He knew that he would not be involved with jade much longer, but it was a fascinating subject and there was no telling when one additional bit of information might be the key to a major conclusion.

He read for almost an hour and a half before he finally went to bed. Even while he slept there were a number of people who wanted very much to get in touch with him; only the fact that his private phone was unlisted made it possible for him to rest undisturbed.

CHAPTER 15

By nine-thirty in the morning the adolescent day was already garbed in its Sunday best, as fine a product as southern California could produce. It was warm and bright; the high shining sun promised rebirth to everyone and everything, and the air was rich with sensuous warmth. Like several million others, Virgil Tibbs took pleasure in it; he sat in his venerable dressing gown, a constant companion of his leisure hours, on his davenport with the window behind him wide open. The freshness and peace of the new day filled his apartment with its welcome exhilaration; it declared that everywhere men were brothers and that nothing but good inhabited the world. That was how the day had been born and if its high ideals were to be defiled, then it would take the weaknesses of the human race to do it.

Unfortunately it was almost a mathematical certainty that somewhere someone had already fouled it up. Some festering domestic quarrel had erupted into violence, a number of automobiles had already been stolen in the small hours of the yet unborn day, perhaps even murder had been done. And in secret laboratories violently dangerous and illegal drugs were being brewed for profit and the degradation of those unfortunates who would use them. Every morning the whole of humanity was staked to a fresh start, but invariably blew it before the first rays of the sun could inch their way above the horizon.

Which was why policemen came to be in the first place.

Virgil read *Peanuts* and was amused; happily there was no visible limit to Charlie Brown's ability to assimilate disasters and survive them unharmed. The sports page announced that the California Angels had acquired a new pitcher who showed unusual promise. The Dow Jones Industrial Average was up a modest amount for the week. And savagery and compassion met head on in a story about a Vietnamese child who had had both legs blown off by a Viet Cong land mine; a picture showed him under specialized medical care in an American hospital.

In the local news section there was an extended article about the sudden, almost inundating pressure that had been brought to bear on all of the hospital and treatment facilities that dealt with drug addiction. A fresh supply of Methadone had been flown in, but there was still a drastic shortage of beds and other essential requirements. Three deaths, apparently from overdoses of an unspecified narcotic, were reported; to Tibbs they were murder.

He got up and poured himself some more coffee. It was instant, but it would do.

His phone rang, which probably meant bad news — it usually did. As he had expected, it was the watch desk. "A couple of things, Virg," the duty man reported. "On the operation which we've got going for you — nothing."

"Thanks, and please don't let up now; there may be a little more happening later on."

"We won't: Lieutenant Olsen left those instructions. Also, a Miss Yumechi Nagashima, or something like that, has been calling you. Do you want to talk to her?"

"I'll call her; I've got the number."

"Right. Have a nice day."

He was in no hurry to talk to Yumeko; he had been enjoying his leisure too much. He thought of going to church, but prudence dictated that he stay close to his phone. Things could start breaking at any time.

Then he picked up his phone and dialed — there might be some news. Chin Soo answered, to be followed very quickly by Yumeko on an extension. "We wish you to tell us what to be doing," the girl said. "We are alone now and we are not sure."

At that precise moment the solution to one of the

most persistent problems that had been nagging him sprang, like Minerva, full-blown out of his brain. He could have shouted "Eureka!" but he restrained himself. "I'm coming over to see you," he said instead. "I'll be there in forty minutes." With that he hung up and turned to the task of shaving and making himself presentable to go out. The last thing he did before leaving his apartment was to close the window; it might be some time before he would be home again and the painting on his wall, if nothing else, was valuable.

Outside the day was fully as fine as he had expected that it would be. As he unlocked his car he thought of at least half a dozen things that he would very much like to do on his precious day off. He had long promised himself to visit the new art museum some day. A good workout at the karate *dojo* would be a sound safeguard against any approaching flabbiness; if he didn't keep in shape Nishiyama would take it out of his hide — literally. He hadn't been to the beach for months — possibly more than twelve of them. And he had yet to ride the Palm Springs tram. He climbed in behind the wheel, fastened his seat belt snugly — because he had seen too many accidents where heads had gone into windshields with gory results and began to drive toward the Wang house, where duty called.

Yumeko greeted him in a blue and white dress that had about it the air of a little girl — one who had grown up and become increasingly feminine in the process. Chin Soo appeared within seconds; he was wearing a short-sleeved shirt and the same trousers that he had had on the night before. Also the same shoes. "I have been working in the jade room," he said.

The house was quite warm. "May I take off my coat?" Tibbs asked.

"As much as you like," Yumeko answered.

That reminded him of something. "You sound like Linda," he said. "The girl whose picture you saw in my apartment. She once wanted me to take all of my clothes off."

"That you would do this I believe; that you would speak of it I do not." Her lower lip crept out a little.

Tibbs looked at her for a moment or two. "Do you know what a nudist park is?" he asked.

"That is yes."

"All right: she lives in one. I went there to look into a homicide — on a hot day beside the swimming pool."

"I hope that the water was nice," Chin said.

Virgil lifted his shoulders slightly and let them fall. "I was on duty. I didn't go in."

Soo proved his intelligence by changing the subject. "I have prepared some boxes as you asked. I have made the cushions very soft so that almost any of the jades could be put in one of them and it would look right."

"Good work," Tibbs said. "Did you check the padding?"

Chin looked at him a little coolly. "Of course."

For a moment Virgil became the teacher. "I assumed that you had, but I always check everything twice if I can. That is the only way to be sure."

The houseboy bowed. "I have lost face," he acknowledged, "and I deserve to. What are your wishes now?"

"There's some work to be done and I will need your help. In the jade room. And I will need Yumeko's permission to handle some of the jades."

"Please to do," she said.

"Thank you — I'll be very careful." He took off his coat and dropped it on a chair. Chin immediately picked it up again and hung it in the hall closet over a wooden hanger. "In that way we do not advertise that you are here," he explained.

Tibbs studied him for a second or two before he spoke. "Let's call it a horse apiece; you're right about that. Are you free to help me now?"

"Let us begin." He led the way toward the rear of the house. At the door to the jade room he paused while he produced a clutch of keys and fitted the right one into the door. "These belonged to Mr. Wang," he said. "I hope that it is right for me to use them."

"He trusted you, didn't he?" Virgil let the question stand as an answer. As soon as the lights were turned on he walked into the jade room and looked about. As far as he could see by an initial inspection, there was no evidence that anything had been disturbed. He turned. "I'd like to get out all of the boxes, then I'll show you what comes next."

"Yes, sir." The houseboy squatted down and opened the bottom of one of the display cabinets. "I have already checked many of them — that is what I was doing. I can give you some information."

"Please do."

"The forbidden drug, there is not as much of it as I thought. The boxes for the older pieces, I mean the pieces that have been here for the longest time, are innocent. Only recent shipments contained it, and even then not all of the boxes, only some."

"How many?"

"I cannot say, sir. I have not examined them all yet."

"Did you mark the ones with the drug?"

"I did not mark them, no sir, but I can tell them."

"How?"

"When I put them back, I stacked those that are ordinary with the pins to the right. The others face the opposite way. It is the way that all of the piles look, so I do not believe that it will be noticed."

Tibbs considered Soo carefully for a few moments. "I told you that I like to double-check things," he said. "I asked you before if you had had training and you denied it. Would you like to reconsider your answer?"

"At the present time I wish only to be instructed by you what you wish me to do," Chin replied.

At that moment Yumeko appeared in the doorway. She looked a question mark at Tibbs, but said nothing. "Come in," he invited. "This is a good time to talk to both of you."

He took hold of the edges of the table that stood in the middle of the room and issued his instructions. "First of all, if anyone — and I don't care who it is — asks you about the jade collection, neither of you knows too much about it — is that clear?"

He received two silent nods in reply.

"Furthermore, if the question arises, you will say that I have advised you to pack the jades away in a safe place for the time being. That is, as soon as convenient after Mr. Wu has had a chance to examine the collection. And Mr. Nakamura."

"Is Mr. Nakamura a reliable person?" Chin asked.

"I consider him so. The people who employ him certainly are."

"We are to admit him, then?"

"If and when he calls — yes. Now the next thing: because you do not know too much about the collection, you will have to do considerable sorting of the boxes to find the right one for each carving."

"I am beginning to understand," the houseboy said, "but please go on."

"I intend to. I want you to get the boxes out — I'll help you — and line them up in front of the cabinets so that the positions of the boxes correspond to the jades on display. You are preparing to pack the collection away for safe keeping."

"But any visitor would know immediately which box is for which jade," Chin observed. "It is a brilliant idea."

"Just once I am going to allow myself this luxury," Tibbs responded. "Elementary."

"It is not so good, I think," Yumeko said.

Tibbs was mildly annoyed. "Why?"

"If it comes somebody who is wishing only the boxes, it will be too easy for them to just take them all. Then you discover nothing."

After a short pause Chin spoke. "In China we used to drown the surplus of female babies shortly after birth. It saved much inconvenience later on."

Yumeko clasped her hands and lowered her head. "Please pardon intrusion," she said.

"She's giving you the Oriental put-on," Chin declared.

"I know — but she's right. So we check the boxes for contents and then stack them back — but in order inside the cabinets." Virgil squatted down and looked inside several of the sections. "That ought to make it hard enough to prevent a mass grab for them all."

"We have work to do," Chin said. "Yumeko can prepare us food."

"That isn't necessary."

"It is good for her, let her do it. We have plenty."

"Perhaps later."

It was slow and tedious work; the supply of boxes seemed almost endless and each one had to be investigated carefully. Those which were innocent had to be put back in good order, a task that Chin assumed while Virgil patiently probed each of the blue boxes and a few that were covered in a bright type of brocade. Yumeko offered her help, but for well-considered reasons of his own Tibbs did not desire any more assistance. When at last the final box had been checked and an accurate tally was possible, twenty-eight caches of the fearful narcotic had been found — enough to add up to something more than a hundred pounds in weight.

That should have been a good enough day's work for anyone, but unfortunately much more still lay ahead. Declining the offer of a meal, Tibbs left the house with the promise that he would be back again before seven.

Before he did anything else he drove straight home, stripped off his clothes, and showered thoroughly just to banish from his mind the idea that any of the damning drug could possibly be on his person. After that, and feeling much more like himself again, he dressed in a quiet dark suit, slipped his gun into its holster, and allowed himself to anticipate the idea of a good dinner.

To get one he drove to one of the best restaurants Pasadena had to offer and allowed himself to be guided to a quiet corner table which suited his mood perfectly. There he let the atmosphere soothe his spirit while he ate prime rib and reflected on the better things of life that everyone should be allowed to enjoy, even if only at intervals. When he had finished his coffee and a sense of well-being surrounded him, he paid his check, reclaimed his car from the attendant, and then headed back to where the painful call of duty awaited him. He was not looking forward to the evening.

Halfway to his destination he stopped at a phone booth and called in to the duty sergeant. "If things work out there may be a little more action at the Wang place tonight," he reported. "You might let the guys on the stakeout know."

"Will do. Any instructions?"

"You might pass the word that if I turn on the porch light, that will mean that I need help. I'll check it after I go in to be sure it's in order. If I can't do that, then I'll try to throw something out a window. The house has heavy drapes that are almost always closed, so that may not work out. Who's going to be there?"

"Out front, Sanderson and Garner. In back, Thistle and Harnois."

"Outstanding. Pass the word that if there's any doubt, they can play it by ear, but not to get jumpy. I'm after proof of guilt."

"Understood; I'll pass it on. Nakamura wants to know if you need him tonight; he's home and available."

"I'll call him on the land line if I do; I have the number."

"Fine. Good hunting, Virg."

"Thanks. Ten four."

Once more he parked his car well away from his destination and continued on foot. The stage was set now; there was little more that he could do except to wait and see if his careful web-spinning was going to produce any results. This was no simple case of murder, if there was any such thing, and the complications which confronted him made matters several times more difficult. He comforted himself with the thought that he could but try, and then rang the doorbell.

Yumeko admitted him. As soon as he was inside she looked up at him as though she was about to say something, but remained silent. Her appearance suggested an idea and he pondered it for a moment. "Would you like to get out of here this evening?" he asked. "It might be a good idea if you were out of the way. I can arrange a comfortable place for you to stay."

She shook her head. "I want to be here. I am female, I know, but I do not wish to be absent."

"All right, but I want you to keep entirely out of the way, upstairs in your room. Don't turn on any lights and keep absolutely still — no matter what happens. Is that clear?"

"That is yes."

"Good." He looked at her sternly. "If you interfere in any way, Yumeko, it will be very serious — do you understand that?"

"I understand."

"You'd better. Now go on up, take off your shoes, and lie down. That's the best thing. And if you hear any noises down here, don't get any sudden ideas or go to the bathroom."

"I will be still."

"That's fine." He turned to Chin Soo, who was close by. "You can be excused if you like — this is a police matter."

The houseboy spoke calmly. "No thank you, sir. It is also my responsibility and I wish to be here."

"Very well, but you will remain quiet."

"My shadow, sir, will make more noise than I will."

"I hope so. Now get this: you are to do nothing, nothing whatever, unless you see me move first — is that clear?"

"Very clear, Mr. Tibbs."

"I trust that we may have some company before the night is over. But I am most anxious to see what takes place before we do a thing. This house is supposed to be empty."

"One question, sir: if I see that you are taking some action, then may I have a piece of it?"

Virgil did not want to commit himself on a firm answer to that. "Exercise judgment," he directed. "Too much help can be as dangerous as too little at some times."

"I understand. May I suggest, sir, that you remove your shoes."

"I intend to."

"I beg your pardon."

"Forget it; now listen." Carefully he spelled out his orders to the houseboy; when they had been delivered he required that they be repeated back. As he was listening, he measured his own physique and training against the lithe figure of Chin Soo. He accepted fully the statement that the young man before him was highly skilled in *Gung Fu* and with his build he could be extremely fast. He did not expect that he would be coming to grips with the younger man, but he was leaving nothing to chance. He had his gun, of course, but he was disinclined to use it except as a last resort. Accurate and effective aim under emergency conditions was always difficult and dangerous — innocent people could get hurt — or worse. And it was not up to him to administer justice with a bullet unless he literally had no choice. Of course if someone else fired first, or tried to, that was different; he certainly had the right to protect himself, and the community.

When he had finished with his briefing he checked the porch light and made sure that it was functioning properly. If Chin Soo understood the purpose of that maneuver he gave no indication; he stood by quietly waiting. Yumeko had gone and there was no sound from upstairs.

In the dining room, which was set off on the right side of the house, there was a mother-of-pearl inlaid Chinese screen. Tibbs carefully placed a small chair behind it and then adjusted the position until he could sit comfortably and still peer out through the narrow vertical slot formed by two adjacent panels. The position was a good one since it allowed him to see a portion of the small entrance foyer and, at a fairly sharp angle the other way, the door of the jade room.

When he had finished Chin touched his arm. "I also have a place," he said. He led the way to the door of the study which was ajar. "I will wait behind here. I do not think anyone will want to come into this room."

Tibbs weighed that and decided that the gamble was a good one. "I don't think anyone will either. In any event, I'll be on hand."

"I am not concerned, sir. It is fortunate that from here I will be able to see where you are."

Virgil stepped behind the door and checked through the crack on the hinged side. The view was adequate and the line of sight covered the corner of the dining room where he would be. He would have much preferred to have had a police officer stationed inside the house with him, but there was an excellent reason why he had chosen Chin Soo instead. Furthermore, he was satisfied that the houseboy had not figured that point out yet, despite the fact that he had demonstrated a definite ingenuity. It would be much better if he did not know.

Tibbs had been on stakeout many times, often when it had been possible to move around a bit, sometimes when, as now, he had had to remain quiet and still.

Before he took up his position he removed his shoes and put them where they were well out of sight. With a short, silent prayer that Yumeko would remain as quiet as she was at the moment, and that Chin Soo would not somehow blow the show, he sat down behind the screen and composed himself. Presently the houseboy moved almost like a disembodied spirit into the study and positioned himself behind the door. Virgil had not suggested a chair for him: if he wanted one he would get it. He tested his own once more to be sure that it did not creak when he stood up, hitched his trousers up a little to make himself more comfortable, and then began his vigil. Hopefully, it would not be an extended one this time; if someone was coming, it should not be too long.

Twice during the following hour he was forced to bestir himself a little to relieve muscle cramps in his body, but he saw no indications that Chin had felt a similar need. One thing at least was going well — the girl upstairs was entirely quiet and there was a reasonable chance that she would remain that way.

At eleven minutes after nine he caught the sounds of someone approaching the house. Very shortly after that the doorbell rang, loud and clear through the still house. For one unnerving moment Tibbs was fearful that Chin Soo would be stupid enough to answer it, then he remembered the intelligence that the houseboy had shown and the careful instructions that he had given to him. When the bell rang a second time he waited and listened: it could be an innocent caller who, having come as far as the front door, was not going to go away without ringing despite the darkness of the house.

A good minute after the second ring there was a small series of scraping noises from the front door. They lasted for only a few seconds, then despite the darkness, the door could be seen opening inward. At that moment, Virgil felt a quick sense of satisfaction; he had a clear and provable case of breaking and entering if nothing else, which solved one immediate problem. He had plenty of reliable witnesses, since the two agents on stakeout covering the front of the house would have been certain to have observed the entry.

More by sound than by anything he determined that two persons were entering the house, presumably both males. He almost prayed that they were not casual burglars, then he knew immediately that that could not be the case. Most forced entries were made from the rear, through a window or some similar means. No, these were men who had confidence in themselves and who had a definite purpose in mind.

In a few seconds the door was shut from the inside, and the darkness was close to complete once more. There was nothing but silence for almost too long a time, then a voice spoke and the pencil beam of a pocket flashlight came to life. It darted about experimentally, checking that the draperies remained tightly closed, then turned toward the back of the house.

Another voice came, this one clearer, and for the second time within a two-minute interval Tibbs felt a sharp stab of satisfaction. The language was not English. It could easily have been Chinese; if so Chin would understand what was being said. Which was the reason why he had used the houseboy in preference to a trained and completely reliable officer.

The thin light began to move toward the rear of the house, accompanied by audible footsteps despite the carpeting. The next quick worry was that the intruders would check out the den; against that possibility Virgil rose silently to his feet and loosened his gun in its holster. He had no intention of firing it as of that moment, but it might have to be displayed, and with convincing speed. He intended to give himself all of the odds that he could.

A long breath flowed silently out of his lungs when the tiny beam of light picked out the door of the jade room and then shortened as the man holding the thin battery case came closer. The door was locked, but Tibbs had satisfied himself early in the afternoon that anyone who knew his business would find that no challenge. His theory in that regard proved right; while one man held the light the second, still invisible in the shadows, worked with a thin strip of plastic against the jam. It took him hardly ten seconds to have the door open.

At that point a decision was necessary; since he could not see inside the jade room from where he was,

Virgil very much wanted to move to a location where he could. But the risk was considerable; a very slight noise could give him away and it followed that if he stood where he could see in, it would be possible for the traveling light to pick him out at almost any time. There was only one sensible answer: to stay where he was and to depend on his ears for evidence as to what was going on.

He heard the bottom sections of the jade cabinets being opened; when he had identified the sound beyond any question he measured once more the angle of the jade room doorway and reminded himself of the exact location of the light switch outside. He balanced on the balls of his feet, ready, but still waiting until one more thing could be established.

He heard brief conversation from inside the jade room and once more concluded that the language was Chinese, but he would have to rely on Chin Soo for a translation of what he had heard.

Then came another sound, one which he knew well as a result of his afternoon's activities — the sliding out of the jade boxes from their hiding place. That did it; ghost-quiet in his stocking feet he moved out from behind the screen, and remaining close to the wall where he could not be seen from within the jade room, he worked his way to a position to one side of the open doorway. With the tips of his fingers he located the light switch, that accomplished he reached inside his coat and very quietly drew out his handgun. He already had a case and he had it in spades, but it was still not enough to satisfy him. He knew what he wanted and at slight additional risk he was confident that he could get it.

The sounds, which were much closer now, told him that the men inside the jade room were working smoothly and rapidly; since they were reported to be professionals, they would understand the importance of minimum exposure. An inquisitive neighbor might have seen them go in and it was barely possible that that same person could have made a call to the police. It was highly unlikely unless the house was also known to be empty, but the risk was there nonetheless and no one but a rank amateur would take any more of a chance than was absolutely necessary.

Abruptly Virgil heard and identified a new sound: someone was picking up boxes and was about to come out. There was a slight pause while his companion, who held the light, apparently took one or two himself, then the moment for action was at hand.

Once more, despite the gun in his hand, Tibbs found the light switch and rested his hand lightly against the wall. As he took a final quick look across the room he was surprised to see that Chin Soo was also pressed against the wall on the opposite side of the doorway; he had not heard the slightest sound of movement from that direction.

The first man came out of the door, the small light outlining him and the stack of boxes he was carrying.

Tibbs drew a deep breath, held it and waited a second or two more until the second man was also out of the jade room. Then he moved his little finger downward on the switch and flooded the room with light.

"Freeze!" he barked, and held his gun squarely aimed at the first of the two men.

Almost instantly the other man whipped his arm around and hurled the box in his right hand directly at Tibbs' face. Virgil ducked barely in time; one sharp corner of the box still caught him on the cheek and gashed the skin. For the better part of a second and a half he was off balance and impotent.

At that same moment he saw the body of Chin Soo already in the air; he had thrown himself up and sideways, feet toward the intruder who was still moving from his throw. From a horizontal position almost five feet in the air Chin kicked out with stunning force: the edge of his shoeless foot hit the side of the jaw so hard that the man's head was snapped around almost ninety degrees. His knees unlocked as his body became a nerveless mass of flesh and bone.

The man in front was almost as fast; he dropped the boxes he had been carrying and thrust his hand inside his coat. From his crouched position Virgil sprang forward and drove his shoulder into the man's armpit. He saw the quick sight of an emerging gun as he seized the wrist and barred the arm across his shoulder, then bent his body forward with all the power he could command. It carried his opponent up and across his back like a giant swing; the man's feet hit the ceiling as he went over, then his body crashed onto the floor with an impact that made the room shake. As soon as he hit, Virgil cocked his right leg and rammed a downward thrust kick which drove the sole of his foot into the man's abdomen, forcing the breath from his body. It was not a lethal blow, but it rendered the man helpless until he could recover enough to pump a fresh supply of air back into his lungs. Meanwhile Virgil bent down and quite calmly picked up the gun with which the intruder had been armed.

Chin Soo spoke behind him. "I was coming to help," he said, "but you did not require it."

"You did your bit," Tibbs answered. He was aware at that moment that he had dropped his own gun; he started to reach for it, but Chin picked it up and handed it to him. "I'll watch them," he added. "Turn on the porch light, please."

Chin turned toward the door. "I believe your friends are already here," he stated; within a few seconds he was back with Sanderson and Garner close behind him.

"We have some customers," Virgil announced dryly. "Take them in and book them for breaking and entering, armed robbery, and resisting arrest. They may not understand English, so take Mr. Soo here with you to act as interpreter."

The two police agents expertly applied handcuffs to their prisoners and relieved the second of them of a gun concealed under his left armpit. They waited patiently until their charges were once more able to get onto their own feet, then Garner took the first one by the arm. "Will you please come with me, sir," he said, and steered him toward the door.

Chin turned. "I do not desire to leave," he declared.

"I understand," Tibbs said, "but please do. I'll look after things here for a little while."

Still Soo hesitated. "The one who comes next will be the most dangerous, I think. And your face is bleeding."

"I am fully prepared," Virgil answered. "You will be needed to translate. Those two must have their rights explained to them."

Chin scoffed, but remained silent on that point. "Very well," he conceded, and followed Sanderson, who was already out of the front door.

It was quiet then in the house. Yumeko gave no evidence of her presence upstairs, although she could not have failed to have heard the noise and the smashing impact when the man Tibbs had thrown had hit the floor. At least she knew how to obey orders.

Calmly Virgil picked up the boxes and in two trips restored them to their approximate positions in the jade room. Then he picked up the tiny flashlight that one of the men had dropped and tested it. It still worked very well within its limitations, which suited him perfectly. He snapped off the light, then went to the front door and made sure that it was still unlocked.

CHAPTER **16**

McGowan looked up from his desk to acknowl-
the man who stood in the doorway of his office.
e in, Virgil," he invited, and put down the pen
as in his hand.

il Tibbs had a sheaf of paper in a folder. "I
e information you wanted on the Chinese nar-
roduction," he said.

wan waved him to a chair, then came from
is desk to join him in the social corner of his
'd like a briefing," he declared. "I'm going
eeting early this evening where the topic is
come up." He relaxed and prepared himself

consulted his notes. "Very well, sir. Starting
he communist Chinese began carrying for-
ry aggressive program of illicit narcotics
, including heroin, which, as you know, is

After that, with the aid of the miniature light he went
into the jade room and closed the door behind him.
Between two of the display cabinets there was a single
chair; he pulled it out and placed it against the far wall
where he would have free movement, but still be out
of a direct line from the door. He sat down with a
sense of gratitude for a few minutes of semicomfort
and respite, but he did not allow himself to be deluded
into a false sense of security. He could not afford it.
He had enough now on the two Chinese strong-arm
types to take them out of the picture for a considerable
time and after that they would probably face deportation. But that did not by any means complete his case.
So he sat quietly in the darkness and waited, surrounded as he knew by an invisible wonderland of
some of the most exquisite art objects to be found in
the world — and something better than a hundred
pounds of one of the most deadly addictive drugs
known to man. The contrast was not lost on him, and
as he thought he reflected on the fact that the attempted theft had been aimed at the crystalline evil
and not at the almost inhumanly beautiful and intricate jades that represented a fortune in themselves.

He sat for more than three quarters of an hour,
alone with his thoughts, wondering why things shaped
themselves the way that they did, until he heard a
slight sound. A single person had entered the front
door, but this time the carpeting muffled any indications of further movements. Virgil sat very still, his

hands in his lap, his breathing steady and even. He remained that way when the door to the jade room opened and someone came invisibly inside, and he was ready when without warning the room lights came on. He could not help squinting because he had been in the dark for so long, but otherwise his composure was unruffled.

"Good evening, Mr. Harvey," he said.

He had to admire the way in which the stock trader accepted the shock. He hardly turned a hair. "Good evening, Mr. Tibbs. What brings you here at this hour?"

"I was waiting for you, sir."

"I see. My coming here uninvited is a legal infraction, of course."

"Yes, it is."

For a second Harvey weakened enough to draw a very deep breath and then let it out slowly. "I am a gambler, Mr. Tibbs," he said finally. "I gambled that you had been fully satisfied."

Virgil remained seated, and said nothing.

The seconds passed through the room in slow precision as neither man changed his position, or spoke. Then, finally, Harvey broke the silence. "Why did you wait here for me like this?"

"Because I needed proof. I was quite confident that you would gamble."

"Are you placing me under arrest?"

"Yes, I am."

"On what charge?"

"For the moment, breaking and entering."

"All right," Harvey said. "I see no need the agony. Can we go now?"

Tibbs rose to his feet. "Before we do, I w ask you just one question."

"Yes?"

Virgil looked at the rich red carpeting and then up again. "I would like to drove that jade stone knife into Wang when you thought that he was already d

Bob
edge
"Com
that w
Virg
have th
cotics p
McG
behind
office. "
into a n
likely to
to listen.
Virgil
in 1951 t
ward a v
production

purely a drug of addiction with no known medical value whatever. In very round figures communist China has about one quarter of the world's population but does less than one percent of the international trade. As a means of developing more foreign exchange, and also weakening potential enemies, they capitalized on the growing market for drugs."

He turned to another page in the papers he was holding. "There are now factories for the production of heroin and other narcotics at Peking, Tientsin, Dairen, Mukden, Chinchow, Kupehkow, Yenki, Shanghai, Hankow, Chungking, Kunming, and a number of other major cities. Within China these plants are known as 'special products processing factories.' During 1970 they produced more than ten thousand tons of illicit drugs which were exported to the free nations through Cuba, North Vietnam, North Korea, Albania, and a number of African nations."

"Did you say ten thousand *tons*?" McGowan asked.

"Yes, sir, that's the figure. Do you want some more?"

"Please."

Tibbs went back to his notes. "According to Kao Hsiang-kao of the Institute of International Relations, this trade reached a volume of approximately eight hundred million dollars annually as of 1970. Of course some of this was intercepted; in 1969, which is the latest report available, the authorities in Hong Kong confiscated more than five tons of opium, two hundred and fifty pounds of morphine, and three hundred and ten pounds of heroin, all from communist China. That's only one port, of course, and there's no way of telling what percentage of the total shipments this represents. What gets through is very specifically aimed at certain nations, and we top the list."

"Damn," McGowan said.

"That's putting it mildly, sir. I'm beginning to appreciate the position that Frank Lonigan and George Duffy are in; the Bureau of Narcotics and Dangerous Drugs has a fearful responsibility."

"Yes, with a flow of more than two million dollars' worth a day. Anything we can do to help them, Virgil, I want it done." He went to the door and asked his secretary to bring in some coffee. When he sat down once more his thoughts had changed somewhat. "Now fill me in on the Wang case," he directed.

Virgil laid aside his notes. "It was sticky because it wasn't simply a matter of who killed Cock Robin. Not long ago the Chinese communists came up with a new product: a synthetic drug that outdoes heroin in both euphoric properties and addiction. A victim caught in the grip of this narcotic would be enslaved, to the point where his life would be ruined. The Chicoms were most anxious to introduce this fearful drug into this country, so they looked for a method to smuggle in steady quantities without using any of the usual dope routes. They hit on the scheme of using jade boxes; the carvings themselves are so compelling they were sure that no one would pay attention to the boxes. It was the stage magician's misdirection applied in a new manner."

He paused while the coffee was brought in, then continued. "Wang Fu-sen was a thoroughly honorable dealer in jades; but without his knowledge or consent he was set up to become a link in the chain. Jades are individual and each one has its own fitted box. By sending pictures of the jades in the loaded boxes to a suitable agent here, he could then buy them and acquire the drug as well. After that the boxes could be unloaded and the jades resold — they have a ready market here despite the prices."

McGowan drank some of his coffee, and continued listening.

"Of course it would all have been much easier if Wang Fu-sen had consented to cooperate, but when he was tentatively approached he firmly refused. Subsequently he let it be known to certain other Chinese-Americans that he was under pressure. They promptly arranged a bodyguard for him and began their own investigation."

"Why didn't they come to us?"

"I have found, sir, that they very much tend to handle their own affairs. Meanwhile, on a trip to the Far East Mr. Wang met Miss Nagashima and realizing that her situation in Japan was a most unhappy one, he brought her back with him. It was personal generosity and nothing more; she returned it by helping to look after his house and by providing a companionship which, while platonic, he much appreciated. The terms of his recent will make that very clear.

"Now about Mr. Harvey. He is, or was, a stock trader who made his living for some time through speculation. But when I examined the records of his stock transactions, I discovered that like a great many others, he had badly misjudged the heavy and sustained bear market of 1969 and 1970. He sometimes held short positions, but he knew that that is a dangerous game and tried to guess the upturn instead. He lost most of his financial resources and capped it by getting into a bitter confrontation with his wife; his position became, for him at least, almost untenable.

"In near desperation he looked for some field where he could make a fast and near-certain profit, legal or not. Through channels which I frankly haven't traced yet he got into the fringes of the narcotics trade. I suspect he made his initial contacts through gambling associations; he admitted to me that he is an inveterate gambler. Gambling and narcotics have been shown to have close connections in many instances. With his remaining capital he began to finance shipments from Mexico and within a few weeks he realized some sharp gains. However, the Mexican narcotics trade had been penetrated by the Chinese communists and through that connection they were able to get to him. He was approached with an inviting proposition which offered steady substantial profits at apparently very little risk:

all he had to do was to appear as a jade collector, and to phone in certain tips he would be given on heroin shipments. Even if the roof fell in on the whole thing, it would be almost impossible to prove anything against him — and that part was perfectly true.

"So Harvey began, but he made a serious mistake right at the beginning — he underestimated the intelligence of Wang Fu-sen. He was instructed to buy certain jades, but his apparent, too-rapid choices from a magnificent stock aroused Mr. Wang's suspicions. In view of the pressure to which he had already been subjected, Mr. Wang put two and two together, reasoned it out, and discovered the secret of the boxes. The next time that Harvey called, Wang gave him a simple choice: stop immediately or the whole thing would be reported to us.

"Harvey told his contacts and they in turn promptly imported two Chicom enforcer types via fake passports and tourist visas to deal with the matter. They called on Wang and attempted to frighten him into silence and cooperation. He calmly refused — and then made a new will. Not too long after that he was killed."

"Which is where you came in."

"Yes, sir, but despite the fact that the case had complications, a few things were apparent from the beginning and they led to the eventual solution. When I first saw the body of Mr. Wang, I could not help noticing the way in which it lay. The arms were at the

sides and it was face up at a thirty-degree angle to
the jade cabinets. It was manifestly impossible for anyone to be stabbed and then to fall into that position, so
despite the fact that a stone knife, or something resembling one, was deeply buried in the chest, I ques-
tioned it immediately as the cause of death.

"Also the deceased had been a slender, frail man
and to drive such a weapon into him while he was
standing would have been all but impossible: he would
either have fallen backwards from the force before
such penetration could be achieved or he would simply have collapsed in a heap. The only logical inference was that the knife had been driven in *after the
body was lying on the floor*. That was quite possible,
because the floor itself would have provided the necessary backing. There is a vast difference between a very
sharp, slender stiletto, for example, and the stone
weapon that was used and which, I know now, wasn't
really a weapon at all."

"Wait a minute, I want to get some more coffee,"
McGowan said. Once more he went to the door and
signaled. "How did you get onto Harvey?" he asked
when he came back.

"At first, pure luck, later on by a process of elimination. When I started in on this case I didn't know the
first thing about jade, but it would have taken a blind
man not to be impressed by the magnificent display in
Wang Fu-sen's home. Despite the fact that I had the
owner's dead body lying on the floor and demanding

my attention, the jades were fascinating; I had never seen anything like them before.

"I picked up an immediate lead to Donald Washburn, whom I had just met that afternoon. I called on him promptly and discovered two things: that he had a very genuine interest in jades and a narcotics problem within his own family. I didn't really tie in the narcotics angle, however, until I discovered that our friends Lonigan and Duffy had been to see Miss Nagashima and apparently had given her a pretty hard time. That was plainer than a letter to Santa Claus and the possibility, even the likelihood, that the deceased had been a dope dealer was right there in front of me.

"As you know, I'm not overly impressed by character references, but I was subsequently interested in the fact that everyone whom I interviewed, without exception, gave him top marks for good character, and the people concerned were of a high level of responsibility — Aaron Finegold for example. Of course that left Miss Nagashima to be considered and you can believe that I considered her. Particularly when I discovered that she had failed to mention the houseboy to me over a period of several days. And there were some other indications.

"I admit that I was quite interested in Mr. Washburn at first, but it didn't fit. His own son was an addict under treatment. Also he was working with the Bureau of Narcotics and Dangerous Drugs and had their implied endorsement. Lastly, he had the laboratory facilities to make keto-bedmidone himself and in fact did, so importing it didn't add up to reality.

"Johnny Wu also displayed a considerable knowledge of jade and interested me until, somewhat by accident, I met Mr. Harvey. As soon as I had contact with him I knew that I had hit pay dirt."

"How?" McGowan asked.

"In the first place I delivered a valuable and very lovely jade to him, but he was remarkably disinterested in it. He hardly looked at it before he put it aside. That seemed very strange. Next, after I had introduced myself as a police officer and specifically told him that I was working on the Wang murder, he pretended almost complete disinterest in the deceased and continued to patronize the hell out of me. That's about as far as you can get from rational behavior; most people are only too glad to clear themselves if they are anywhere near a homicide and aren't responsible for it."

"Granted. Anything else?"

"Yes. In view of the very casual way he had treated his new acquisition I made it a point to ask him if he had taken a long time in its selection. He answered me, 'No, I never require time to make up my mind. That's one of the basic principles for success in the market.' The hell it is; nobody has snap judgment that good. And who would look at more than a hundred magnificent jades and then pick one out as though it were nothing more than a candy bar?"

"So you had him pegged at that point."

"No, sir, not entirely, but I was interested enough to ask to see his jade collection. Any normal collector would be eager to display his acquisitions, but Harvey first wanted to know if it was necessary. When he finally did show me his supposed treasures, he had them in his office, twelve of them, in a case where they were lined up like so many lead soldiers. I studied them for a little while just to give him a chance to tell me about them, but he didn't have a word to say. As a jade collector he was a total miscast; he wouldn't have convinced a schoolchild. Later on I made it a point to look at several other private collections: the Finegolds', the Washburns', and Johnny Wu's. All of them were tastefully arranged and the owners were delighted to display and talk about them. The question then was: why was Harvey buying jades when he so obviously was disinterested in them? Possibly for investment purposes, but that would be over a period of time and it was out of character for him to deal in fine art objects. When I learned about the drugs in the jade boxes, I didn't have to look any farther for an answer. But, dammit, I couldn't prove anything! I knew that he had knowledge of the murder, if murder it was, but I had no way to put the screws on him. Then, at last, I found out about the two strong-arm types that were loose in town and the picture began to shape up."

"Is that why you set up a stakeout and threw a party with Bob Nakamura in the role of a jade buyer?"

"Yes, sir, of course. I remembered something Harvey had told me. He said that he made his money taking advantage of the amateurism of many small investors who have no clear idea of the market or what they are doing. I thought that it might be profitable to reverse that principle and take advantage of his lack of understanding of homicide investigation. If I could get him to reveal himself, even to a minor degree, then he might construe that as meaning that it was all over and lower his defenses. It worked. I set him up for an apparently dead-safe breaking and entering which he might easily have beaten in court if he had wanted to contest it. So right at that point I asked him a question that was calculated to trigger him into thinking that it was all over. He fell for it and that was that."

Bob McGowan stretched his long legs and for a few seconds contemplated the toes of his well-shined shoes. Then he looked again at Tibbs. "So Harvey murdered Wang Fu-sen."

"No, sir, he didn't."

"Now wait a minute — I don't follow you."

"I'll try to clarify it. The two hard cases we have in custody called on Wang Fu-sen and beat him up, trying to force him to remain quiet and cooperate. They throttled him, knocked him senseless, and left him lying on the floor. That's firm and established. He might have been dead at that time, but I seriously doubt it: the medical evidence will tell us one way or the other."

"I'll assume that he was still living."

"Good. Now Harvey may be ruthless, but he isn't stupid. The Chicoms take no chances and while he had played ball all the way, if Wang talked, he was in for it. So he didn't have to think very hard to figure out who would be the next to be silenced. Himself. He knew what was going to happen, so he went to the Wang house himself to find out the score. He was safe, he thought, he was presumably coming to buy jade. He found the door open, went in, and discovered Mr. Wang lying on the floor. He mistook him for dead. In that desperate moment he had the idea that he could get rid of the two Chinese by pinning it on them; by making it look like a ritual killing or a tong murder. A lot of people still believe in those things, you know. He found one cabinet unlocked; Wang had been rearranging the contents. The stone knife, or what looked like a knife, was there. He took it and drove it into Wang's chest. In my opinion, that's when Wang was killed, but because Harvey thought that the man was already dead, it was technically accidental homicide and not murder. The intent to kill wasn't there, or if it was, we can never prove it."

"You told me it wasn't simple," the chief said.

"Someday, sir," Tibbs said, "I want to investigate a murder done in an English country house over the weekend with only six persons present and the outside roads impassable because of a sudden storm and flood. One where the victim is found in a locked room with an arrow through his heart and there isn't any question of multiple assault or lack of premeditation."

McGowan shook his head gravely. "I've heard of that case," he said. "The butler did it."

Tibbs shrugged his shoulders. "Now you've spoiled all my fun."

"Not quite. Miss Nagashima was in to see me earlier today. You can do me a favor if you will — pick her up at four o'clock . . ." he glanced at his watch ". . . fifteen minutes from now at the parking lot across the street and drive her home. Then call it a day."

"I was going to see her anyway, sir. There's a little detail I want to discuss with her."

"Fine, you do that. Did Harvey talk?"

"I managed to persuade him that it would be in his best interests to be candid with us."

"One last question: where are the jade boxes with the dope in them?"

"Downstairs in narcotics."

"Good. Go get Miss Nagashima."

"Yes, sir."

Virgil cleared the top of his desk by putting things into a drawer that had served that purpose before, said good-night to Bob Nakamura, and went out to collect his passenger. He used his own car to pick her up; she climbed in silently and sat beside him. He remained quiet too until they had cleared the immediate downtown traffic, then he spoke to her. "Yumeko, you know what you did, don't you?"

She lowered her head. "Yes," she whispered.

"Why didn't you tell me?"

She fumbled with a miniature handkerchief, then swallowed hard. "I don't know," she answered.

"Chief McGowan almost asked me and if he had, I would have had to tell him."

"I know."

He guided the car around a corner and slowed down for the residential street. "If I hadn't studied that jade book, I might have been in trouble."

"Yes." She did not look up.

"All right, Yumeko, why did you put those four jades on the floor around Mr. Wang's head?"

When she looked up there were tears in her eyes. "You know," she answered. "You ask me if we have any funeral jades and I say no."

"But you're Japanese."

"Half," she corrected.

"If you want it that way. But why?"

She wiped her eyes. "I want to do him honor. I know we have no funeral jades to put on his tongue and in his ears, so I make honor for him that way."

"All right, but why didn't you tell me that?"

Again she lowered her head. "I don't know."

He left her alone after that until he pulled up in front of her house. "Here you are," he said.

She laid a hand on his arm. "Please to come in one minute," she asked. "I have reason."

He followed her up the steps and through the foyer

after she had unlocked the door. "Chin Soo is gone," she explained.

"Permanently?"

"No, not yet."

She patted her hair into place and stole a glance in the hall mirror; then she led the way toward the rear of the house. From her purse she extracted the ring of keys that had been Mr. Wang's and opened the door to the jade room. It looked very much as it had before as soon as she turned the lights on; the serenity of the rare objects that it contained belied the violence that had happened there.

She fitted a cabinet key and slid back the glass panel. Then she took out the mutton fat vase with the intertwined branches and flowers that she had used when she had lectured to him about jade. She held it out. "This is for you," she said.

Virgil shook his head clearly and at once. "No, police officers cannot accept gifts. It's magnificent and thank you, but no."

Yumeko did not move. "I know this, so I ask McGowan sensei and he give special permission. You can ask him."

"Yumeko, thank you again, but I'm afraid that I can't."

"You accept picture of beautiful naked girl. Also valuable."

Because she was still holding it out he took the magnificent carving from her and held it in his hands for several seconds. Then he set it down carefully on the table beside him and moved a step away.

"A police officer cannot accept a gift," he repeated.

She picked up the jade and moved until she was directly in front of him. "It is not a gift," she said. "It is bribe."

"Bribe! Do you know what that means?"

"Yes, I know. I also tell Mr. Chief McGowan that I bribe you."

"I don't get it," Tibbs said.

She lifted his hand and laid it against the jade. "This is bribe and you take it. I want you to become my boyfriend."

"But you don't have to bribe me to do that." Still slightly upset, he spoke without thinking.

She smiled at him. "Good you say so!"

He looked at her — at her Japanese features and her dark Negro skin. Then he made the mistake of looking at her eyes and was held there. "You will do?" she asked.

"Put down the jade," he answered, "and we'll see."

THE PERENNIAL LIBRARY MYSTERY SERIES

Ted Allbeury

THE OTHER SIDE OF SILENCE   P 669, $2.84
"In the best le Carré tradition . . . an ingenious and readable book."
        —New York Times Book Review

PALOMINO BLONDE   P 670, $2.84
"Fast-moving, splendidly technocratic intercontinental espionage tale
. . . you'll love it."   *—The Times* (London)

SNOWBALL   P 671, $2.84
"A novel of byzantine intrigue. . . ."*—New York Times Book Review*

Delano Ames

CORPSE DIPLOMATIQUE   P 637, $2.84
"Sprightly and intelligent."
        —New York Herald Tribune Book Review

FOR OLD CRIME'S SAKE   P 629, $2.84

MURDER, MAESTRO, PLEASE   P 630, $2.84
"If there is a more engaging couple in modern fiction than Jane and
Dagobert Brown, we have not met them."   *—Scotsman*

SHE SHALL HAVE MURDER   P 638, $2.84
"Combines the merit of both the English and American schools in the
new mystery. It's as breezy as the best of the American ones, and has
the sophistication and wit of any top-notch Britisher."
        —New York Herald Tribune Book Review

E. C. Bentley

TRENT'S LAST CASE   P 440, $2.50
"One of the three best detective stories ever written."
        —Agatha Christie

TRENT'S OWN CASE   P 516, $2.25
"I won't waste time saying that the plot is sound and the detection
satisfying. Trent has not altered a scrap and reappears with all his old
humor and charm."   *—Dorothy L. Sayers*

Andrew Bergman

THE BIG KISS-OFF OF 1944   P 673, $2.84

"It is without doubt the nearest thing to genuine Chandler I've ever come across. . . . Tough, witty—very witty—and a beautiful eye for period detail. . . ."
—Jack Higgins

HOLLYWOOD AND LEVINE   P 674, $2.84

"Fast-paced private-eye fiction."
—San Francisco Chronicle

Gavin Black

A DRAGON FOR CHRISTMAS   P 473, $1.95

"Potent excitement!"
—New York Herald Tribune

THE EYES AROUND ME   P 485, $1.95

"I stayed up until all hours last night reading *The Eyes Around Me*, which is something I do not do very often, but I was so intrigued by the ingeniousness of Mr. Black's plotting and the witty way in which he spins his mystery. I can only say that I enjoyed the book enormously."
—F. van Wyck Mason

YOU WANT TO DIE, JOHNNY?   P 472, $1.95

"Gavin Black doesn't just develop a pressure plot in suspense, he adds uninfected wit, character, charm, and sharp knowledge of the Far East to make rereading as keen as the first race-through." —Book Week

Nicholas Blake

THE CORPSE IN THE SNOWMAN   P 427, $1.95

"If there is a distinction between the novel and the detective story (which we do not admit), then this book deserves a high place in both categories."
—New York Times

END OF CHAPTER   P 397, $1.95

". . . admirably solid . . . an adroit formal detective puzzle backed up by firm characterization and a knowing picture of London publishing."
—New York Times

HEAD OF A TRAVELER   P 398, $2.25

"Another grade A detective story of the right old jigsaw persuasion."
—New York Herald Tribune Book Review

MINUTE FOR MURDER   P 419, $1.95

"An outstanding mystery novel. Mr. Blake's writing is a delight in itself."
—New York Times

THE MORNING AFTER DEATH   P 520, $1.95

"One of Blake's best."
—Rex Warner

A PENKNIFE IN MY HEART P 521, $2.25
"Style brilliant . . . and suspenseful." —*San Francisco Chronicle*

THE PRIVATE WOUND P 531, $2.25
"[Blake's] best novel in a dozen years . . . . An intensely penetrating study of sexual passion. . . . A powerful story of murder and its aftermath."
—Anthony Boucher, *New York Times*

A QUESTION OF PROOF P 494, $1.95
"The characters in this story are unusually well drawn, and the suspense is well sustained." —*New York Times*

THE SAD VARIETY P 495, $2.25
"It is a stunner. I read it instead of eating, instead of sleeping."
—Dorothy Salisbury Davis

THERE'S TROUBLE BREWING P 569, $3.37
"Nigel Strangeways is a puzzling mixture of simplicity and penetration, but all the more real for that."
—*The Times* (London) *Literary Supplement*

THOU SHELL OF DEATH P 428, $1.95
"It has all the virtues of culture, intelligence and sensibility that the most exacting connoisseur could ask of detective fiction."
—*The Times* (London) *Literary Supplement*

THE WIDOW'S CRUISE P 399, $2.25
"A stirring suspense. . . . The thrilling tale leaves nothing to be desired."
—*Springfield Republican*

Oliver Bleeck

THE BRASS GO-BETWEEN P 645, $2.84
"Fiction with a flair, well above the norm for thrillers."
—*Associated Press*

THE PROCANE CHRONICLE P 647, $2.84
"Without peer in American suspense." —*Los Angeles Times*

PROTOCOL FOR A KIDNAPPING P 646, $2.84
"The zigzags of plot are electric; the characters sharp; but it is the wit and irony and touches of plain fun which make the whole a standout."
—*Los Angeles Times*

John & Emery Bonett

A BANNER FOR PEGASUS   P 554, $2.40

"A gem! Beautifully plotted and set. . . . Not only is the murder adroit and deserved, and the detection competent, but the love story is charming."   **—Jacques Barzun and Wendell Hertig Taylor**

DEAD LION   P 563, $2.40

"A clever plot, authentic background and interesting characters highly recommended this one."   *—New Republic*

THE SOUND OF MURDER   P 642, $2.84

The suspects are many, the clues few, but the gentle Inspector ferrets out the truth and pursues the case to its bitter and shocking end.

Christianna Brand

GREEN FOR DANGER   P 551, $2.50

"You have to reach for the greatest of Great Names (Christie, Carr, Queen . . .) to find Brand's rivals in the devious subtleties of the trade."   **—Anthony Boucher**

TOUR DE FORCE   P 572, $2.40

"Complete with traps for the over-ingenious, a double-reverse surprise ending and a key clue planted so fairly and obviously that you completely overlook it. If that's your idea of perfect entertainment, then seize at once upon *Tour de Force.*"   **—Anthony Boucher, *New York Times***

James Byrom

OR BE HE DEAD   P 585, $2.84

"A very original tale . . . Well written and steadily entertaining."
    —Jacques Barzun and Wendell Hertig Taylor, *A Catalogue of Crime*

Henry Calvin

IT'S DIFFERENT ABROAD   P 640, $2.84

"What is remarkable and delightful, Mr. Calvin imparts a flavor of satire to what he renovates and compels us to take straight."

        —Jacques Barzun

Marjorie Carleton

VANISHED   P 559, $2.40

"Exceptional . . . a minor triumph."
    —Jacques Barzun and Wendell Hertig Taylor, *A Catalogue of Crime*

George Harmon Coxe

MURDER WITH PICTURES   P 527, $2.25
"[Coxe] has hit the bull's-eye with his first shot."

—*New York Times*

Edmund Crispin

BURIED FOR PLEASURE   P 506, $2.50
"Absolute and unalloyed delight."

—Anthony Boucher, *New York Times*

Lionel Davidson

THE MENORAH MEN   P 592, $2.84
"Of his fellow thriller writers, only John Le Carré shows the same
instinct for the viscera."   —*Chicago Tribune*

NIGHT OF WENCESLAS   P 595, $2.84
"A most ingenious thriller, so enriched with style, wit, and a sense of
serious comedy that it all but transcends its kind."

—*The New Yorker*

THE ROSE OF TIBET   P 593, $2.84
"I hadn't realized how much I missed the genuine Adventure story
. . . until I read *The Rose of Tibet*."   —Graham Greene

D. M. Devine

MY BROTHER'S KILLER   P 558, $2.40
"A most enjoyable crime story which I enjoyed reading down to the last
moment."   —Agatha Christie

Kenneth Fearing

THE BIG CLOCK   P 500, $1.95
"It will be some time before chill-hungry clients meet again so rare a
compound of irony, satire, and icy-fingered narrative. *The Big Clock* is
. . . a psychothriller you won't put down."   —*Weekly Book Review*

Andrew Garve

THE ASHES OF LODA   P 430, $1.50
"Garve . . . embellishes a fine fast adventure story with a more credible
picture of the U.S.S.R. than is offered in most thrillers."

—*New York Times Book Review*

THE CUCKOO LINE AFFAIR   P 451, $1.95
". . . an agreeable and ingenious piece of work."   —*The New Yorker*

A HERO FOR LEANDA P 429, $1.50
"One can trust Mr. Garve to put a fresh twist to any situation, and the ending is really a lovely surprise." —*Manchester Guardian*

MURDER THROUGH THE LOOKING GLASS P 449, $1.95
". . . refreshingly out-of-the-way and enjoyable . . . highly recommended to all comers." —*Saturday Review*

NO TEARS FOR HILDA P 441, $1.95
"It starts fine and finishes finer. I got behind on breathing watching Max get not only his man but his woman, too." —Rex Stout

THE RIDDLE OF SAMSON P 450, $1.95
"The story is an excellent one, the people are quite likable, and the writing is superior." —*Springfield Republican*

Michael Gilbert

BLOOD AND JUDGMENT P 446, $1.95
"Gilbert readers need scarcely be told that the characters all come alive at first sight, and that his surpassing talent for narration enhances any plot. . . . Don't miss." —*San Francisco Chronicle*

THE BODY OF A GIRL P 459, $1.95
"Does what a good mystery should do: open up into all kinds of ramifications, with untold menace behind the action. At the end, there is a bang-up climax, and it is a pleasure to see how skilfully Gilbert wraps everything up." —*New York Times Book Review*

FEAR TO TREAD P 458, $1.95
"Merits serious consideration as a work of art." —*New York Times*

Joe Gores

HAMMETT P 631, $2.84
"Joe Gores at his very best. Terse, powerful writing—with the master, Dashiell Hammett, as the protagonist in a novel I think he would have been proud to call his own." —*Robert Ludlum*

C. W. Grafton

BEYOND A REASONABLE DOUBT P 519, $1.95
"A very ingenious tale of murder . . . a brilliant and gripping narrative." —Jacques Barzun and Wendell Hertig Taylor

THE RAT BEGAN TO GNAW THE ROPE   P 639, $2.84
"Fast, humorous story with flashes of brilliance."

—*The New Yorker*

Edward Grierson

THE SECOND MAN   P 528, $2.25
"One of the best trial-testimony books to have come along in quite a
while." —*The New Yorker*

Bruce Hamilton

TOO MUCH OF WATER   P 635, $2.84
"A superb sea mystery. . . . The prose is excellent."
—Jacques Barzun and Wendell Hertig Taylor, *A Catalogue of Crime*

Cyril Hare

DEATH IS NO SPORTSMAN   P 555, $2.40
"You will be thrilled because it succeeds in placing an ingenious story
in a new and refreshing setting. . . . The identity of the murderer is really
a surprise." —*Daily Mirror*

DEATH WALKS THE WOODS   P 556, $2.40
"Here is a fine formal detective story, with a technically brilliant solution
demanding the attention of all connoisseurs of construction."
—Anthony Boucher, *New York Times Book Review*

AN ENGLISH MURDER   P 455, $2.50
"By a long shot, the best crime story I have read for a long time.
Everything is traditional, but originality does not suffer. The setting is
perfect. Full marks to Mr. Hare." —*Irish Press*

SUICIDE EXCEPTED   P 636, $2.84
"Adroit in its manipulation . . . and distinguished by a plot-twister which
I'll wager Christie wishes she'd thought of." —*New York Times*

TENANT FOR DEATH   P 570, $2.84
"The way in which an air of probability is combined both with clear,
terse narrative and with a good deal of subtle suburban atmosphere,
proves the extreme skill of the writer." —*The Spectator*

TRAGEDY AT LAW   P 522, $2.25
"An extremely urbane and well-written detective story."
—*New York Times*

S. B. Hough

DEAR DAUGHTER DEAD   P 661, $2.84
"A highly intelligent and sophisticated story of police detection . . . not to be missed on any account."   —Francis Iles, *The Guardian*

SWEET SISTER SEDUCED   P 662, $2.84
In the course of a nightlong conversation between the Inspector and the suspect, the complex emotions of a very strange marriage are revealed.

P. M. Hubbard

HIGH TIDE   P 571, $2.40
"A smooth elaboration of mounting horror and danger."
                                                 —*Library Journal*

Elspeth Huxley

THE AFRICAN POISON MURDERS   P 540, $2.25
"Obscure venom, manical mutilations, deadly bush fire, thrilling climax compose major opus.... Top-flight."
                                   —*Saturday Review of Literature*

MURDER ON SAFARI   P 587, $2.84
"Right now we'd call Mrs. Huxley a dangerous rival to Agatha Christie."   —*Books*

Francis Iles

BEFORE THE FACT   P 517, $2.50
"Not many 'serious' novelists have produced character studies to compare with Iles's internally terrifying portrait of the murderer in *Before the Fact,* his masterpiece and a work truly deserving the appellation of unique and beyond price."   —Howard Haycraft

MALICE AFORETHOUGHT   P 532, $1.95
"It is a long time since I have read anything so good as *Malice Aforethought,* with its cynical humour, acute criminology, plausible detail and rapid movement. It makes you hug yourself with pleasure."
                                  —H. C. Harwood, *Saturday Review*

Michael Innes

APPLEBY ON ARARAT   P 648, $2.84
"Superbly plotted and humorously written."   —*The New Yorker*

APPLEBY'S END   P 649, $2.84
"Most amusing."   —*Boston Globe*

THE CASE OF THE JOURNEYING BOY   P 632, $3.12
"I could see no faults in it. There is no one to compare with him."
—*Illustrated London News*

DEATH ON A QUIET DAY   P 677, $2.84
"Delightfully witty."   —*Chicago Sunday Tribune*

DEATH BY WATER   P 574, $2.40
"The amount of ironic social criticism and deft characterization of scenes and people would serve another author for six books."
—Jacques Barzun and Wendell Hertig Taylor

HARE SITTING UP   P 590, $2.84
"There is hardly anyone (in mysteries or mainstream) more exquisitely literate, allusive and Jamesian—and hardly anyone with a firmer sense of melodramatic plot or a more vigorous gift of storytelling."
—Anthony Boucher, *New York Times*

THE LONG FAREWELL   P 575, $2.40
"A model of the deft, classic detective story, told in the most wittily diverting prose."   —*New York Times*

THE MAN FROM THE SEA   P 591, $2.84
"The pace is brisk, the adventures exciting and excitingly told, and above all he keeps to the very end the interesting ambiguity of the man from the sea."   —*New Statesman*

ONE MAN SHOW   P 672, $2.84
"Exciting, amusingly written . . . very good enjoyment it is."
—*The Spectator*

THE SECRET VANGUARD   P 584, $2.84
"Innes . . . has mastered the art of swift, exciting and well-organized narrative."   —*New York Times*

THE WEIGHT OF THE EVIDENCE   P 633, $2.84
"First-class puzzle, deftly solved. University background interesting and amusing."   —*Saturday Review of Literature*

Mary Kelly

THE SPOILT KILL   P 565, $2.40
"Mary Kelly is a new Dorothy Sayers. . . . [An] exciting new novel."
—*Evening News*

Lange Lewis

THE BIRTHDAY MURDER P 518, $1.95
"Almost perfect in its playlike purity and delightful prose."
— Jacques Barzun and Wendell Hertig Taylor

Allan MacKinnon

HOUSE OF DARKNESS P 582, $2.84
"His best . . . a perfect compendium."
— Jacques Barzun and Wendell Hertig Taylor, *A Catalogue of Crime*

Frank Parrish

FIRE IN THE BARLEY P 651, $2.84
"A remarkable and brilliant first novel. . . . entrancing."
— *The Spectator*

SNARE IN THE DARK P 650, $2.84
The wily English poacher Dan Mallett is framed for murder and has to confront unknown enemies to clear himself.

STING OF THE HONEYBEE P 652, $2.84
"Terrorism and murder visit a sleepy English village in this witty, offbeat thriller." — *Chicago Sun-Times*

Austin Ripley

MINUTE MYSTERIES P 387, $2.50
More than one hundred of the world's shortest detective stories. Only one possible solution to each case!

Thomas Sterling

THE EVIL OF THE DAY P 529, $2.50
"Prose as witty and subtle as it is sharp and clear. . .characters unconventionally conceived and richly bodied forth . . . . In short, a novel to be treasured." — Anthony Boucher, *New York Times*

Julian Symons

THE BELTING INHERITANCE P 468, $1.95
"A superb whodunit in the best tradition of the detective story."
— August Derleth, *Madison Capital Times*

BOGUE'S FORTUNE P 481, $1.95
"There's a touch of the old sardonic humour, and more than a touch of style." — *The Spectator*

Henry Kitchell Webster

WHO IS THE NEXT? P 539, $2.25
"A double murder, private-plane piloting, a neat impersonation, and a delicate courtship are adroitly combined by a writer who knows how to use the language." —Jacques Barzun and Wendell Hertig Taylor

John Welcome

GO FOR BROKE P 663, $2.84
A rich financier chases Richard Graham half 'round Europe in a desperate attempt to prevent the truth getting out.

RUN FOR COVER P 664, $2.84
"I can think of few writers in the international intrigue game with such a gift for fast and vivid storytelling."
—*New York Times Book Review*

STOP AT NOTHING P 665, $2.84
"Mr. Welcome is lively, vivid and highly readable."
—*New York Times Book Review*

Anna Mary Wells

MURDERER'S CHOICE P 534, $2.50
"Good writing, ample action, and excellent character work."
—*Saturday Review of Literature*

A TALENT FOR MURDER P 535, $2.25
"The discovery of the villain is a decided shock." —*Books*

Charles Williams

DEAD CALM P 655, $2.84
"A brilliant tour de force of inventive plotting, fine manipulation of a small cast and breathtaking sequences of spectacular navigation."
—*New York Times Book Review*

THE SAILCLOTH SHROUD P 654, $2.84
"A fine novel of excitement, spirited, fresh and satisfying."
—*New York Times*

THE WRONG VENUS P 656, $2.84
Swindler Lawrence Colby and the lovely Martine create a story of romance, larceny, and very blunt homicide.

Edward Young

THE FIFTH PASSENGER P 544, $2.25
"Clever and adroit . . . excellent thriller. . . ." —*Library Journal*

If you enjoyed this book you'll want to know about
THE PERENNIAL LIBRARY MYSTERY SERIES
Buy them at your local bookstore or use this coupon for ordering:

Qty	P number	Price
————	————	————
————	————	————
————	————	————
————	————	————
————	————	————
————	————	————
————	————	————
————	————	————
————	————	————
————	————	————
————	————	————
————	————	————
————	————	————

	postage and handling charge	$1.00
	———— book(s) @ $0.25	————
	TOTAL	☐

Prices contained in this coupon are Harper & Row invoice prices only. They are subject to change without notice, and in no way reflect the prices at which these books may be sold by other suppliers.

HARPER & ROW, Mail Order Dept. #PMS, 10 East 53rd St., New York, N.Y. 10022.

Please send me the books I have checked above. I am enclosing $_____ which includes a postage and handling charge of $1.00 for the first book and 25¢ for each additional book. Send check or money order. No cash or C.O.D.s please

Name_____

Address_____

City_____ State_____ Zip_____

Please allow 4 weeks for delivery. USA only. This offer expires 1/31/86
Please add applicable sales tax.